Few critics have been a
as William Peden in defe
strengthening the positio.. ᴐᴦ ᴛʜᴇ
short story in American literature.
His book *The American Short Story*
is well known, and he has edited
anthologies and has written count-
less articles and reviews of short
story collections for the *New York
Times Book Review, Saturday Review,* and various literary quarter-
lies.

Now, with this volume of short
stories, Peden makes his own debut
— and an impressive one — as a serious and talented fiction writer.

Some of the stories collected here
have appeared in *Story, The New
Mexico Quarterly, Genesis West,*
and other periodicals.

Peden explores important human
relationships and human loss — loss
of a child, love, youth, physical
grace. Some of his characters are
weak, some talk too much or drink
too much or withdraw from reality,
but all are sympathetic, deserving
of compassion.

Here are stories the discerning
reader will remember and want to
reread, each time with more meaning and a deeper sense of satisfaction.

Night in Funland
and Other Stories

Night in Funland
and Other Stories

William Peden

LOUISIANA STATE UNIVERSITY PRESS · Baton Rouge

For Petch, Eliza, and Sally

Publisher's Note

With this collection the Louisiana State University Press inaugurates a program of regular publication of short stories. Our reason is a simple one—the same reason which earlier prompted some of the university presses to publish poetry: there was a void to be filled. Poetry collections by talented but relatively unknown poets were going unpublished for reasons that were largely financial. It is our feeling, reinforced by talks and correspondence with many writers and editors, that the same thing is now true regarding the publication of collections of stories. It is no secret that the attitude of most commercial publishers is: novel, yes; short stories, no. In a modest way, we hope to help fill the void.

Three distinguished writers and critics have agreed to serve as an informal advisory board to help select the manuscripts most worthy of publication. They are R. V. Cassill, now teaching at Brown University; George Garrett, at Hollins College; and Reynolds Price, at Duke University. Publication of a volume does not imply the unanimous decision of the advisors, however; the final decision on each manuscript is made by the Louisiana State University Press.

Acknowledgments

�֍ Grateful acknowledgment is made to the editors of the publications in whose pages some of these stories first appeared: the *New Mexico Quarterly, Story, Genesis West,* the *University Review, P S: Poems and Stories, The Girl in the Black Raincoat,* and the *Denver Quarterly.* The author is also grateful to New Directions for its kind permission to quote from Dylan Thomas' "A Child's Christmas in Wales," which appeared in *Quite Early One Morning,* 1954, and from "Fern Hill," published in *The Collected Poems of Dylan Thomas,* 1946. The lines from Robert Lowell's volume, *Imitations,* 1961, are reprinted with the permission of Farrar, Straus and Giroux.

Contents

Night in Funland
and Other Stories

Night in Funland

✿   They drove slowly down the highway that cut cleanly through the desert, past the glittering motels with their swimming pools of pale blue water, past the shops of pink or green or azure adobe. In the humming light of the mercury-vapor lamps, the child was a gnome in a pool of color, the shadows beneath her eyes sooty in the darkness that had overrun the mesa. The father reached over and patted her hand. She squeezed his and edged closer toward him.

"Are you sure this is the way, Daddy?"

"Of course it is, Amanda, don't you remember?"

"Well, yes, sort of, but I thought maybe it was the other way."

"The other way is east, goosie," he said; "we go west. Look, in a minute, at the next stop light, we'll see the wheel, and then you'll remember."

At the intersection he slowed down as the traffic light clicked from green to amber and then to red.

"Look . . ." He pointed at the rosy sky. "Over there; can't you see the top of the Ferris wheel?"

She squealed with delight; then the light changed and they left the shining highway, and in darkness that was like a sudden plunge into unknown waters turned onto a bumpy dirt road.

"Can we get there this way?" Amanda asked. "Does this road go through?"

"Don't worry; sure it does, honey. You just wait."

Then they were pulling into the tumbleweed-speckled parking lot. He switched off the motor and turned off the lights and went around and opened her door. Amanda came out slowly, and she smiled up at her spare, slightly stooped father.

"This is fun," she said. She reached for his hand and they walked beneath the arch that spelled out F-U-N-L-A-N-D in winking colored lights. It was a clean bright place, no leg shows, no wheels of fortune, no freak tents with greenish two-headed babies in discolored alcohol-filled jars; a clean bright place on the mesa, bounded by a miniature railroad with puffing steam engine and train of cars. They could hear the whistle now at the far dark end of the park, faraway and thin and clear, and Amanda tugged at his hand again. He wanted to pull her close to him and kiss her and pat her thin hair and tell her how glad he was that she was so much better and they could go on a spree together as they had in the old days, and he patted her hand and buttoned the top button of her sweater.

"Let's sit down a little," he said. His heart was thumping and the palms of his hands were damp.

"Oh, Daddy," she said, "not now."

"You must rest a minute," he insisted; "you must remember this is the first time . . . ."

They sat down on the bench by the small depot, and the train with its bell clanging and its whistle shrilling and its headlight stabbing at the night swung around the turn and stopped quietly almost in front of them. The engineer, a teen-aged boy crouching precariously on the tender, got up to stretch his legs while the young passengers spilled from the coaches.

"What shall we do first?" the father asked. "Do you want to ride the train?"

"I'd like a snowball first," she said. Children were climbing on and off the train like monkeys and he thought there were too many of them and one of them might cough on her or something; it wouldn't help her, God knows, to catch a cold just now. She walked ahead of him slowly, a trace of her old jauntiness in the blue toreadors with the white bows tied neatly just below her knees and the white-trimmed cap on her dark head, past the pool with its boats floating in the oil-dark water, and the enclosure where the ponies awaited their riders, and the clanking fury of the scenic railway.

"This is the nicest park ever," he said, and squeezed her hand. "I've never been in a nicer park, have you, Amanda?"

"No," she said; "it's the nicest ever."

At the refreshment booth he ordered two snowballs with grape flavoring. The efficient girl in her starched white uniform pushed a button and there was a whirling sound, and the ice as white and fine as snow poured through a vent, and the girl scooped it up and expertly without touching it by hand transferred it into paper cups, and then she squirted thick dark purple fluid onto the ice, and it was suddenly, magically, like a sunset transformed into a violet delight, and she smiled and passed the cups over the counter.

"Keep your fingers out of it," he said to Amanda.

They rested on a bench and tilted the cups to their lips, and the sweet ice gushed into their mouths.

"Isn't it good?" Amanda said. "It gets sweeter as it goes down."

"Yes," he said, and thought how few things were sweeter as they got down, and he squeezed his cup and the fluid was bright and clean in his mouth.

"This is the nicest park there is," he said again.

"Yes," she said, and drained at her snowball with a sucking, bubbling sound. She thrust her thin fingers into the cup to extract the last sweet dregs. Roughly he snatched out her hand and slapped her hard, and cried by God he had told her to keep her fingers out of it and did she want to get sick all over again. She flushed and he felt as if he had kicked her, and he pulled her close to him and kissed and stroked her hair; her thinness was like a blow.

"I'm so sorry, honey," he said, "but I've been worried about you. You mustn't mind when I act like this. It's only because I love you so much, and I don't want you to get sick again, ever."

She slowly turned her head towards him, and tried to smile, and he took out his monogrammed handkerchief and brushed at the corners of her eyes.

"Now how do you feel?" he asked, and when she said she felt fine he wanted to shout and dance and sing. He held her hand as they walked away from the refreshment booth while the starched girl squinted at him, and they walked slowly over the hard-packed grayish dirt. There was very little dust, he thought with satisfaction; he had never known a place like Funland to be so clean and orderly.

Amanda suddenly broke from his grasp.

"Oh," she cried, and ran towards a large brightly lighted cage near an open place where baby tanks puffed and grunted.

"Look," she called; "oh, Daddy, look."

In the bright clean cage, littered with a scooter, a tricycle, rubber balls, a trapeze, and a punching bag, a young chimpanzee sat in a baby's high chair, munching at a banana.

"Rollo," the sign atop the cage read, "Just Recently Arrived from the Belgian Congo Region of West Africa. A two-year-old chimpanzee . . . just four and a half months in captivity."

Daintily Rollo nibbled, breaking off small chunks with his long-haired, tiny-nailed hands and placing the fruit meticulously in a mouth like the furnace door of the small train emerging from its tunnel with a triumphant toot and jangle. The chimpanzee finished his treat, placed the parachute of limp skin on the tray of his chair, and wiped his hands on scarlet trousers. Amanda screamed with delight and Rollo swung with dedicated grace to land noiselessly on the floor with flat tennis-shoe-clad feet. With beautiful, strong, pink-palmed hands he grasped the bars of his cage and gazed at the child, stonedark eyes in his clean tan face, and he opened his great lips and smiled.

Amanda clapped her hands and Rollo whirled and leaped to the rope which spanned the cage; hand over hand, he swung from one end of the cage to the other. By ones and twos people approached, laughing and chatting, and Rollo again dropped like a sunbeam to the floor. His trainer, a gentle, patient man with a limp and a face too much like Rollo's to be a coincidence, reached for the roller skates hanging on the wall and attached them to the chimpanzee's high-topped tennis shoes. He held his hand, and Rollo glided noiselessly on his well-oiled skates, skating surely and competently and enjoying himself.

When the man climbed clumsily over the low iron railing in front of the cage and tossed a few pieces of popcorn between the bars, Rollo stumbled and almost fell. The attendant reached quickly for the chimpanzee's hand, and frowned at the intruder. Amanda turned upon the popcorn thrower, a fat man whose hairy black nipples stared blankly beneath a bilge-colored nylon sport shirt.

"You've frightened him," she said in sudden fury. "You've frightened him."

In anger the fat man threw another handful of popcorn between the bars, and the trainer sadly shook his head. Still holding Rollo by the hand, he led him to the high chair and swung him up to the seat, and removed the skates. Then he pulled a switch, and all the lights in the cage went out. Rollo sat alone, his yellow shirt and scarlet trousers and sneakered feet now gray in the darkness.

"Christ," the fat man said. "Who does that guy think he is, anyways? Christ, it's only a monkey."

He grabbed his fat child, a child with a face like a rutabaga, and disappeared.

"What a horrid, nasty man," Amanda said. "Can't we see Rollo again? Won't he come out again?"

"Maybe later," the father said; "maybe later."

"Besides," she said, "he's not a monkey. He's a chimpanzee, an anth . . . anthropoid, isn't he, Daddy?"

"That's right," he said. "He's not a monkey, he's an anthropoid, and maybe he'll come out later anyhow."

Amanda walked away, but soon stopped at the foot of the Ferris wheel. She gazed upwards at its swift smoothness, sparkling, a small circle of lights winking near the hub, and a larger circle glowing in the middle, and the whole great machine alive with an outline of red and blue and green neon tubing, flashing as the twelve carriages, one red then one black then another red and another black, swam miraculously into the cool dry blackness of the starless night, some carriages swinging empty, in another two teen-aged girls singing "Oklahoma," in others a father and a white-faced, pop-eyed infant, a young man and a girl their arms locked around each other as they soared from the light to the darkness, and two boys clowning and roaring. The operator squeezed the grip-handle of the lever and pushed it and the engine slowed down, and the wheel came to a silent stop. There was a sudden, almost reverent hush, and a squeal of terrified delight from the occupants of the carriage at the very top of the wheel swinging coldly in the dark, and then the voices of the girls singing "Oklahoma" clear and far away and miles and miles away in the thin cold air at the top of the wheel, and miles and miles away from the hard gray ground and the prancing merry-go-round horses with their flaring orange nostrils and white champing cannibal teeth and the refreshment stand with the efficient girl in her starched white uniform. The operator stepped on a pedal, and a landing platform slid close to the carriage; the attendant lifted the bar and the occupants stepped gingerly down, the father glad to deposit the child into the mother's arms.

"Must we ride this now, Amanda?" the father asked.

"Oh, yes," she said and edged her way towards the entrance. "Can I," she said, and squeezed his hand, and her dark eyes glistened, "oh, can I go all alone like you promised when I was sick?"

"Let me go with you," he said.

"Don't be a meanie," she said. "Please, Daddy, remember you promised."

"All right," he said. "All right, but you must be very, very careful. You must promise to sit right in the middle of the seat, and you must keep your hands tight on the bar all the time. Do you promise?"

"Brownie's honor," she said and held up her hand, palm outwards and three fingers aloft in a half salute. She hugged him, and he lowered his head and she brushed his cheek with a quick kiss.

The wheel stopped again, and he gave her her money and said loudly, "Give it to the man." He looked at the operator like a fellow-conspirator suddenly catching in a great crowd the long-anticipated signal, and again he said loudly, "If you don't sit right in the middle and hold the bar tightly I shall ask the attendant to stop the wheel."

"Oh, Daddy," she said. The operator smiled when she gave him the money, and placed her firmly in the very middle of the carriage, clicking the protective bar into place with special emphasis as though to say: I understand the way you feel; don't worry.

Amanda sat very straight in her seat and gripped the iron bar. The operator pushed the lever slowly forward, and the wheel rose noiselessly. Amanda smiled from her perch as the operator again pulled back the lever, and the wheel stopped and an aged man and wife emerged from their carriage as though from the floor of the ocean.

Again the operator pushed the lever, and the wheel began to turn. The father ran back a few feet; he could see Amanda tiny, disappearing into the darkness. He hoped the operator would not halt the wheel with Amanda's carriage at the summit. His scrotum tightened as he thought of her, up there alone in the dark. He saw the crouching mountains, a ragged darkness palpable against the blueblack of the night, and the city swimming in a blob of red and blue and green and orange and white lights, while to the west naked and blue the desert scattered its bones to the ends of the vanished watershed. Then Amanda in a black carriage outlined with green neon swept past him and smiled and was gone. He started to wave, but checked his arm, not wanting her to take her hands from the iron bar to reply. Then in what seemed an instant she came by him again, and he winked at her reassuringly before her carriage swam upwards into the darkness. He looked at the sturdy iron wheel and the concrete foundation. This was no fly-by-night carnival, but a permanent operation, thank God, he thought; thousands of people rode the safe, sturdy wheel each season. Again Amanda was smiling when her carriage flashed by, and he lighted a cigarette and smiled conspiratorially at the operator in his white overalls, a sensible man with one foot resting nonchalantly near the flywheel of the generator.

He counted the carriages as they glided before his line of vision, one red then one black, then another red and another black. He awaited the passage of Amanda's carriage which he must have missed while he was lighting his cigarette. Suddenly, painfully, a hard ball of fear exploded in his throat.

This is absurd, he thought. He forced himself to stand still and look with studied calm at the swiftly turning wheel. What had been the color of the tubing which outlined Amanda's carriage. Green? No, red. Surely not red on a red, or was it a black, carriage?

The wheel made several more swift, noiseless circuits, and still he could not see the pale smiling face of Amanda. His hands shook and sweat drenched his back and upper legs. With an effort as conscious and deliberate as holding his breath under water he controlled himself. This is ridiculous, he thought. This is an optical illusion. He said to himself, I will count each carriage very carefully as it goes past, and then I'll see her, and soon the wheel will stop, and she'll get out, and we'll have a very good laugh about this.

He counted the carriages as they glided swiftly before his eyes. First a red with an old man, then two empties, then a black with two grinning nobheaded boys, then a red with the girls now singing "Oh, What a Beautiful Morning," then an empty, then another red, and his heart suddenly soared like a geyser only to sink hideously; it was not Amanda, but a much older child. Then a man and a child and two more empties, then a red with a mother and a baby followed by a black with a soldier and a girl, then another red with an old man, the same hideous old man he'd begun counting with, and with a cry like an animal's he leaped over the low steel railing and clutched at the attendant's arm.

"Stop it," he said, "for God's sake, stop the wheel."

The attendant frowned, then smiled, and squeezed the handle of the lever, and pulled back the lever, and an empty black carriage swung like a dry leaf above his head.

"My daughter," he gasped, "the little one with the black hair," but two dirty-nosed boys pushed their way between him and the operator, poking out their hands with the money in them, and climbed into the carriage snickering and guffawing and wolfing popcorn.

"For the love of God!" he cried, and the popcorn-eaters looked at him as though he were an ape in a straw hat. "For the love of God, where is my daughter? I think it's time you let the little girl off. The one with the black hair. She has on a blue suit and a cap. You remember?"

"Yes sir," the attendant said, and smiled.

Relief flowed through him; he slapped the operator heartily on the back. "I lost sight of her for a moment," he said. "In the dark. My eyes. It gave me a turn, for a moment."

The operator nodded, and pushed the lever, and the next carriage, empty, swung past, and he stopped the wheel at the next to let the mother and baby out. The baby had wet its diaper and a black stain overspread the mother's breast like a wound. Then there was the carriage with the soldier and the girl, and they leaned out and yelled whatsthematterwhyduhyuhkeepstoppinthe-wheel? Then another empty and one in red with the old man, and he lost count.

"Amanda," he screamed. His voice was like a ship sinking darkly. "Amanda," he screamed again, and the attendant stopped the wheel and came towards him and he was no longer smiling. People converged upon him, he was the center of a whirling funnel of blank paper faces.

"Good God, good God," he cried. "Where are you, baby?"

The children in the toy train again making its sliding halt before the depot leaned over the edges of the coaches and looked questioningly at the Ferris wheel glowing in the distance.

"Amanda," the father cried, and the sound tore and twisted its way above the clanking of the scenic railway and the put-put-put of the miniature tractors and the wheezing of the merry-go-round. Noiselessly the curtains of the clean cage parted, and the lights flowed on, and Rollo climbed quietly down from his high chair. He listened intently to the wild broken cries in the night. Then he pressed his tan face against the bars and gazed with comprehending eyes at the dark figure with uplifted head outlined like a corpse against the spokes of the great wheel blazing in the night.

Wherefore Art Thou, Romeo?

❋ "I think it's simply awful," Leila said to Girard, and gingerly sidestepped the crumpled blanket in the pantryway between the cool, high-ceilinged dining room and the kitchen. "It's simply a disgrace the mess that dog makes."

Girard did not answer, but patted his lips with his napkin and pushed aside his half-finished dessert.

Leila looked with distaste at the dog's battered tin dish, incongruous in so handsome a house, with the crumbs of food hardening on the rim. She limped on high-heeled green Capezios to the sink and scraped the remains of an avocado salad from the dark wooden bowl. "And to think we used to let him sleep and eat by the icebox."

"He is a nuisance, to be sure," Girard said. "He *has* become a bit of a pariah in some ways. But a great one," he continued, raising the cultivated voice which still retained traces of the earthy resonance of his tobacco-planting forbears.

"I'm not so sure about the greatness," Leila said, and hastily drained the last drops of the sherry which was all Girard permitted before lunch on the days of his Contemporary Fiction seminar. "I'm not at all sure of his greatness, dear," she repeated, and returned to the dining room.

"Never forget it, Leila," he said as she sat down. Again he raised his voice slightly and regarded her with bright blue eyes. "He's a great dog, as well as one with a celebrated past." He pushed aside the Spode coffee cup and reached for the magazine he had brought with him to the table.

"But he's become such a nuisance. And it *is* discouraging, trying to keep the pantry clean. Ardella scrubs it two or three times a week, and everything looks so nice, but then. . ." Leila wrinkled her nose. "He comes in and the whole house looks like a pigpen." She looked at him thoughtfully. "I think, sometimes, we should have the old boy put to sleep."

Girard slapped the tidy blue cover of the magazine and stared at her angrily.

"Don't bring that up again, Leila," he said, finally. "I dislike Romeo as much as you do, sometimes, but I won't have it. And Roddy would be heartbroken. How can you think of such a thing? Just because he's old, and you think he's a *nuisance*."

She sensed rather than saw his quick, bright, unsmiling glance at her leg as she gingerly sat down.

"Of course, dear," she said. "I didn't mean it literally. Why, I'm as fond of him really as you or Roddy."

She limped around the table and laid her hand gently on his close-cropped, prematurely gray head. Girard's face softened and he patted her bottom, well made and shapely beneath the pale green linen dress. His eyes were half-closed and he studied the immaculate eggshell white of the ceiling.

"It's true, Leila, that he belongs to Winesburg, Ohio, rather than here in Charlottesville. He's definitely become a grotesque. But so have we all, in one way or another, haven't we?"

Instinctively she smoothed the dress along her bad leg.

"What do you mean by that?"

He avoided her eyes. "Sic transit gloria mundi," he said. "Let us remember his youth and forget the present." Again he tilted back his head and gazed at the ceiling. "With rue my heart is laden," he began, but imperious barking interrupted his reverie.

"Oh Lord," Leila groaned, "he wants back in again. And I let him out just before we sat down."

She limped slowly into the living room. At the white brick fireplace she paused for a moment before the still life, its bold splashes of scarlet and gold echoing the rich tints of the oriental rugs and accenting the lighter hues of the draperies. The painting, as usual, was crooked; the century-old house sank slightly to the south. She tipped the lower corner with a manicured index finger and stepped back to appraise the result. At the sound of the dog's impatient whine she frowned, knowing it would be followed by what could be described only as a scream; the dog was indubitably,

Girard often declared, one of the truly great screamers of the present generation.

She opened the door and the dachshund bolted between her legs, toenails rattling on the hardwood floor, and leaped into his bed in the pantryway. From his disorderly sanctuary he regarded her with the bemused concentration of a Rembrandt self-portrait, then lowered his head and noisily began to wash himself.

"Romeo!" Leila's voice was menacing.

The dog cocked his long head and yawned, displaying a mouthful of broken yellow teeth, and resumed his task.

"Stop that, dog!" Leila cried, and shook her finger angrily. The animal returned her stare for a long moment, blinked, and again lowered his head.

"Cease, forbear, and desist," Leila said, in conscious imitation of Girard's rhetoric. Romeo looked up, and she raised both arms above her head, her tapering fingers outstretched in a Dracula-like gesture. The dog made several twisting circuits of his blanket, furiously kneaded the nest with his gnarled paws, and subsided.

"He *is* intelligent." She smiled at Girard. "If only he weren't *so* intelligent."

"He's a tremendous personality, truly. And that's a great act of yours, by the way. You could make a fortune with that on television."

"Don't be silly," she said. "But he's so dirty. Only yesterday Ardella found him simply *writhing* in the garbage. He follows her out everyday like a hyena when she takes the garbage out. I've seen him skulking around the pails like a . . . ."

"Poor old chap," Girard said. "He's hungry all the time. Forbidden sweets, you know."

Again he half closed his eyes and studied the ceiling.
"I'll admit that the medicated dogfood is a constant
expense. But remember the days of his grace and greatness, my dear. He may drop dead at your feet at any
moment, poor fellow. You wouldn't want that, would
you, just because he's old and enfeebled? And a nuisance?"

"Of course not," she said hastily. "Not because he's
old surely. And not that he's a nuisance. It's just that
. . ."

Girard picked up the magazine. "Let's not discuss
him further at this time," he said, in the tone that
meant let's get to something important. Affectionately
he stroked the cover of the magazine. Leila's hands
were beginning to sweat; with a conscious effort she
folded them in her lap, and waited.

"Do you really like the article?" he asked.

"I think it's very good," she said. "Excellent, one of
your very best."

He beamed, and riffled the pages. "That's good of
you, Leila; that's very good of you. How do you like
this passage? I'm rather fond of it myself."

Girard paused for a moment and gazed into space.
" 'The Vision of Sex and Death in the Writings of
Dylan Thomas,' " he intoned, his voice vibrating curiously high as it did so often when he quoted his own
work. He's an intelligent man, Leila silently repri-
manded herself, and a good critic, but that rhetoric!

Girard cleared his throat.

" 'Set in the Jarvis Hills of Wales that Thomas knew
so intimately,' " he commenced, " 'the early short stories are a curious mixture of folklore, fantasy, allegory,
and surrealism. The smell of death is on many of them,

and madness permeates most of them, and the incubus of sex hovers over all of them like a slowly-descending shroud.' "

"That's very perceptive, that last," Leila said. "Sex the tiger, and all that."

"Please, Leila," he said, lifting his hand in protest. "Must you always . . . ?"

"I'm sorry," she said. "Do go on."

He frowned at her ever so slightly before continuing.

" 'These stories are uniquely Dylan Thomas, unique in their intensity, in the prodigality of their rhetoric, in their special kind of hyperthyroid sexuality. The early Thomas may be described as a Welsh Stephen Dedalus with a perverse and decadent sense of humor, an intellectual David Copperfield with an overwhelming interest in female anatomy.' "

Girard reverently closed the magazine and again with scrupulous attention studied an invisible configuration on the ceiling. "Ah," he muttered, "what genius I possessed when I penned that article." He dabbed at the corners of his mouth, glanced at the handsome Omega on his wrist, and yawned.

"God in heaven," he lamented, "I must return to the salt mines soon. I'm doing Tennessee Williams this afternoon." He grimaced. "I must lie down for a few minutes."

He picked up the magazine, paused a moment to pat the top of Leila's head, and retired to the downstairs bedroom. She sat quite still for a moment. Her joints felt like jello, and the slight crawling sensation in her armpits was becoming insistent.

"Wake me in a few minutes if I should doze off," Girard called.

"Of course, dear," she said, and picked up some dishes, and limped through the pantryway. Romeo had turned over and lay on his back, snoring asthmatically. Poor old fellow, she thought, he looks like a plucked chicken, and averted her eyes. Why, she often wondered, did Roddy have to christen him Romeo? And why, having been given such a name, had the dog happened to turn out like *that?* He's all musket and no gunpowder, one of their friends had said after three unsuccessful attempts to mate him, and after that they never tried again.

In the kitchen Leila scraped the dishes and left them on the sink for Ardella. She looked back over her shoulder, and opened the cabinet door and withdrew the bottle with the white-lettered black label. Slowly, lovingly, she poured some whiskey into a shot glass, admiring the slow, golden, sunflecked trickle.

"And how *is* poor Dylan, I wonder?" she called to Girard. "You haven't heard from him lately, have you?"

She continued her skillful, delicate pouring, glorying in the almost imperceptible rise of the liquid in the glass. My favorite game of skill, she thought, my one and only parlor trick. The whiskey approached the top of the glass, reached it, exceeded it, threatening to spill over in aromatic ruin, but at precisely the right second she raised the neck of the bottle and halted the golden flow.

"He's in New York with that jackass Hannum," Girard's voice floated from the bedroom. "Not in good shape, I understand."

"Too bad," she whispered. The bouquet from the brimming shot glass rose warmly to her nostrils and her throat contracted. God bless our happy land, she thought, and imagined endless cornfields, golden as a Van Gogh landscape, ripening under a burning sun with the quickening smell of harvest in the dry air. Ritualistically, without spilling a drop, she transferred the liquor to a tall glass, marveling as she always did at her steadiness of hand. She added some ice and picked up the rectangular bottle. She gazed at it a moment before sloshing additional whiskey over the ice; only then did she raise the glass to her own blurred image in the kitchen window.

"Ahhh, that's good," she said, half aloud, after a long swallow. "God bless the distillers of America. And God bless you, too," she continued, admiring the sturdy, dependable-looking bottle. "A thousand and one blessings on thee."

"What are you saying?" Girard called. "What are you mumbling about?"

"Nothing, dear," she replied, drinking rapidly. "Nothing at all. But you must get up soon or you'll be late for class."

A groan from the pantryway interrupted her. She took a swallow and walked into the passage, hobbling ever so slightly. You walk beautifully, the poet had told her when they had had many drinks after his reading at the University; you walk as though you had a guinea egg tucked between your legs, and with no preliminaries he had put his plump, nailchewed hand up her dress (Girard having passed out quietly some moments before) , and with no resistance she had let him take her on the couch: Do not go gentle into that good night, she had said.

"What is he doing in New York?"

Romeo groaned again, and turned over. Dozing there

with just the ragged tips of his teeth visible beneath his
graying muzzle, he looked like an Old Testament patri-
arch. Moved by sudden compassion she leaned over to
pat him, but the thick dark smell which rose from his
old body arrested her hand and she looked automatically for the opened green bottle on the ledge above his
head. How long had it been since she had petted him or
played with him—he the runt of a purebred litter, vel-
vet-soft, so shy he would turn away his head when she
or Roddy approached his flannel-lined basket, or would
lie for hours half hidden in her beloved flower garden,
with only the black tip of his long nose visible, or the
gleam of his dark eyes. Poor old chap, she thought, and
bent over again and rubbed his dry muzzle.

"Remind me to get some more Airwick," she called
and quickly straightened up. "I declare, this dog is becoming intolerable."

She finished her drink, rinsed the glass, and quickly
poured another. Poor lovely Dylan. Poor sweet unhappy little man.

"What is he doing in New York?" she called again,
and took a long, long swallow. She had driven him to
the airport and on the way out they had stopped at a
motel; your belly is a great poached egg, he had
laughed; surely you can do better than that, she had
said, and they had missed the plane: had Girard known,
she had wondered, but it no longer mattered. She
smiled and took another long drink, delighting in the
warm, slow return of sensation to her legs and stomach.

"You'll be late if you don't hurry," she called. "Is he
going on another of those awful lecture tours?"

In the pantry, she almost stumbled over Romeo, who

had pulled his blanket from the wall and lay outstretched in gasping slumber. With difficulty she retained her balance.

"Awake, caricature," she said, and nudged him with her toe. The dog opened one eye and raised his head.

"Out, my sick friend," she said. "Out!"

Grumbling, he opened his other eye, stretched elaborately, yawned, and stretched again.

She raised her arms above her head and pointed in the direction of the front door. "Up, up, and away!"

The dog disentangled himself slowly; then, as though freed from a net, he broke into a run; she winced at his scratching halt at the front door, the thud of his body and his triumphant bark as the door slammed. She returned to the kitchen and finished her drink.

"I'm leaving the article in the bedroom," Girard called from the front hall. "Yes, another lecture tour for our poet. New England this time. See you around five."

She poured more whiskey into her glass, and sipped it while she tidied up the kitchen. Her chores finished, she locked the back door (Ardella will not come till four, good old Ardella, and Tuesday is Roddy's Cub Scout day) and freshened up her drink before locking the front door.

In the sunny bedroom she drew the venetian blinds, kicked off her shoes, and lay down on the bed. She pulled up her skirt and lay quietly for several minutes, and thought of the night at the Charlottesville motel and how they had both laughed at the bright green socks he had bought at the airport in Kansas City and how, later, he had suddenly and uncontrollably wept as they lay in the great bed and watched the moonlight scatter luminous mice on the wall-to-wall carpeting. I will have to read the article before Girard gets home, she thought, but there'll be plenty of time for that, plenty of time. She arose unsteadily, took another sip of her drink, and walked to the record cabinet. Romeo was scratching and whining at the front door; she toyed with the idea of calling up the vet. After her disastrous fall from the horse, she had begun to dislike the dog intensely, but when the vet told them he had a kidney ailment and would be better off destroyed she had suddenly decided no, let's try to keep him alive as long as we can, and they had put him on the expensive medicated dogfood, and he had outwitted all of them by living, by becoming more and more demanding, a grotesque, all bones and hide and limp phallus.

"Wherefore art thou, Romeo, indeed?" she said.

The scratching at the door had subsided, so she took from the record cabinet the first of Dylan's recordings (he read his own work like an angel, a fallen angel) and carefully removed the disc. She scrutinized the shiny surface carefully, and softly blew at the invisible wash of dust. She placed the record on the spindle and flipped the switch, and lay back on the bed. As the poet's voice flooded the room, she again pulled up her skirt. The words, the music of the rich voice, the intensity of the poet were warm as mulled wine; they flowed through the room like tidewater.

Nothing I cared, in the lamb white days,
    that time would take me
Up to the swallow thronged loft by the
    shadow of my hand,
In the moon that is always rising,

Nor that riding to sleep
I should hear him fly with the high fields
And wake to the farm forever fled from the
*   childless land.*
Oh as I was young and easy in the mercy of
*   his means,*
* Time held me green and dying*
Though I sang in my chains like the sea.

Will you write to me? She had asked him. Of course, he had said, but she knew he never would, and then he had gone home to Wales, and now here he was back in America, getting ready for another round of lectures and lionizings and exhaustion and conquests and sickness and the terrible fright which seemed never to leave him. *Sleep is lovely,* he had quoted that night; *sleep is lovely, death is better still, not to have been born is of course the miracle.*

His voice faded away and the record changer clicked off. She rose unsteadily from the bed and turned the record over.

One Christmas was so much like another, the bardic chanting began, and she opened the blinds. Full October sun bathed their lawn in a golden glow which reminded her of her favorite Rousseau, the oil painting of four moustached men tossing an eggshaped football against a background of Indian-summer warmth and ruddy trees. *Years and years ago, when I was a boy, when there were wolves in Wales,* the voice continued, and her cheeks were warm with sudden tears.

Poor Dylan, poor dear Dylan, will I never see you again?

She picked up her glass and stood uncertainly for a

moment before limping through the dining room, golden now like the lawn, to unlock the back door. Soon Ardella would amble in to prepare dinner, and Roddy, excited with talk of cookouts and scout tests and square knots, and finally Girard, elated as always after a successful seminar or moody and irritable if things hadn't gone well.

She *would* read the article. He would want to discuss it after dinner. He would be both hurt and difficult if she hadn't read it. Slowly she walked to the front door and opened it. She gasped, and stepped back, hand pressed against her open mouth. Romeo lay sprawled on his back on the doormat, his mouth agape, the arch of his hairless chest motionless.

He's dead, she thought; my God, he's dead.

Her heart suddenly twisted. She hurried back to the kitchen as fast as her leg would permit, and picked up the whiskey bottle and took a long swallow.

"What will Roddy say?" she said. "Whatever will he say? I'll have to get the vet here before he gets home from scouts."

She took the telephone from the kitchen wall, started to dial a number, hesitated for a moment, and replaced the receiver. She tiptoed back to the front porch and looked at the body on the doormat. Was there a slight tremor along the graying muzzle? She could not tell. Cautiously she nudged him. The old body did not move. She nudged him again, more firmly this time; when he suddenly started she drew back her foot as though she had almost stepped on something foul half hidden in dry sand, and relief and disappointment broke inside her simultaneously. She nudged him again and the dachshund arose slowly, extending each hind-leg by turns and shaking it as though it had been water-drenched; he arched his body like a gymnast, his chest almost touching the floor, and rose and looked questioningly at the door.

Leila leaned over and patted the dry, bony head; her fingers played with his ears, as worn and creased as the leather of a workingman's glove.

"Give 'em hell, McGillicuddy," she said, and opened the door. I'll have one more drink before reading the article, she thought, just a very small one. The poet's voice followed her into the kitchen, singing of Christmas and Useless Presents and Auntie Hannah who liked port. Soon, she knew, he would finish and the record player would turn off.

I'll make a pecan pie. Girard and Roddy used to love my pecan pies.

How long, she tried to remember, how long had it been since she had baked a pie? She ticked off, slowly, the ingredients—brown sugar, butter, Karo syrup. Brown sugar, butter, Karo syrup . . . and, of course, pecans. It was quite likely that there were no pecans in the house. She looked around the kitchen aimlessly. Where was the small stepladder? How could she search the shelves for pecans if she could not find the stepladder? She ran her fingers hopelessly through her hair and took another long swallow of whiskey.

"It would be impossible to make a p'can pie without p'cans," she declared to the wall. "Quite impossible." She sat very still on the stool and listened to the chanting voice in the bedroom.

Looking through my bedroom window, out into
the moonlight and the unending smoke-colored snow,

I could see the lights in the windows
of all the other houses on our hill and hear
the music rising from them up the long, steadily
falling night. I turned the gas down, I got
into bed. I said some words to the close and
holy darkness, and then I slept.

When the record player turned off, the quiet house seemed cold and empty. Leila placed her glass on the sink and laid her head on her arm. Not possible to make a pie, she thought. She decided fuzzily to do nothing, to sit out the remainder of the afternoon, to wait very quietly in the kitchen, to do nothing at all but wait until she heard Ardella's comforting footsteps at the back door.

Easter Sunday

✤ It is a sunny morning in Queensville and in the grassy quadrangle formed by five or six white-pillared fraternity houses a group of medical students, engaged in some extra-curricular surgery, are screaming happily. The scent of mint and bootleg corn whiskey lingers in the warm air, and the quadrangle is littered with the artifacts of an all-night party—an overturned piano, many empty or partially-emptied Mason jars, white gloves, high-heeled shoes, a baseball bat, embroidered evening bags, a garter belt, two recorders, a zither, a collapsed opera hat, innumerable lipstick-stained cigarette stubs, a book of poems by Dorothy Parker, one package of condoms, and a water buffalo which the medical students have recently removed from the zoological museum of the University. At the cloven hoofs of the water buffalo lies the passed-out body of a young man, Tiny Jim Atkins, five feet two inches tall, Southern Conference three-meter diving champion, and currently a medical student and president of his class.

Gradually the screams of the students penetrate the drawn window shades of a front room on the second floor of one of the white-columned buildings. In a rumpled bed a young man, also a medical student, awakens slowly and in pain. His head is ringing like a Chinese gong and his mouth feels as foul as ditch-water. Warily he opens one eye and recoils in horror at the sight of the gaping mouth, cruel yellow teeth, wrinkled snout, and hate-filled eyes of a wildcat about to spring.

"God in heaven," he mutters, and closes his eyes and braces himself against the warm body next to him: *what is that thing doing here?* Then he remembers. The cat, too, has been recently pilfered from the zoological museum. Relief flows through him and he turns over and puts one shaking arm around his companion's shoulder. She awakens slowly, makes small burrowing movements in the bedclothes, and mutters something unrecognizable but pleasant; then she reaches for one of his hands and they lie quietly for a few moments.

Again the cries of the medical students disturb the silence. The girl opens her eyes, runs her fingers through her thick auburn hair, and yawns.

"What's going on out there, Peter?"

He groans; the walls of his skull seem to be contracting and expanding and when he moves his head he feels as though he were about to fall from some great height. He tries to rise from the bed but the effort is costly. I'm going to throw up, he thinks, and lies back and closes his eyes.

The shouts are louder, more gleeful now, and the girl climbs over him and tiptoes to the window and cautiously pulls the shade to one side.

"My word," she says.

The sourness in his stomach seems to have subsided slightly, so he carefully opens his eyes and looks at the girl.

"What's all the racket about?" he asks and immediately closes his eyes and bites his lips to keep the bile from rising in his throat.

"They're cutting up a water buffalo, or about to."

"They're *what?*"

"They're cutting open a water buffalo."

"Oh," he says, and turns over and starts to go back to sleep. The girl tiptoes back to the bed, carefully avoiding the evening dress, handbag, and underwear on the floor.

"What's that?" he cries suddenly. "Did you say they're cutting open a water buffalo?" His eyes are still closed but he is beginning to feel better again.

"Yes," she says, and returns to the window. "A water buffalo. And they're doing a mighty good job of it, too."

"Who are?"

"Your good friends. Your buddies. Taggart and Peyton and, oh, the whole bunch of them."

"Strange," he says. "I don't see why they would cut open a water buffalo." He looks at the ceiling. "Could you get me a little drink? Maybe just a short one."

She walks to the desk and searches for the Mason jar among the mess of books, papers, cigarettes, clothes, half-filled glasses, and a microscope. Her body is trim and beautiful and tanned. She has just returned from a vacation in Bermuda and her legs and shoulders are coffee-colored against the whiteness of her torso. How beautiful she is, he thinks, how very beautiful.

"Here it is," she says, loud against the cries from the quadrangle, pointing to the Mason jar.

"Shhhhh," he says, holding an index finger to his lips. "Not so loud; somebody may hear you."

She smiles and raises one hand palm upwards and shrugs her shoulders in a gesture of gentle exasperation. She pours two or three inches of the pale, straw-colored fluid, and hands him the glass; then, as the cries from the quadrangle increase in intensity, she returns to the window.

"Amazing," she says, half to herself.

"What's amazing? What's going on out there now?"

"They've cut open the buffalo."

"Oh?"

"Yes, they've cut him completely open."

"They could get in trouble . . . ," he begins, but her sudden gasp cuts him short.

"Oh, they shouldn't," she says. "Oh, they mustn't do that. That's horrid!"

"Shouldn't what?" he mumbles drowsily. "What's horrid?"

Then she is standing over him, shaking his shoulder roughly.

"Get up, get up this very minute! You mustn't let them do it."

"Do what?"

"Just get up!" she cries. She takes his hand and half drags, half leads him to the window and pulls back the shade.

"Look," she points. "Just look. Oh, Peter, you must do something."

With difficulty he narrows his eyes; slowly, painfully, his vision clears. The buffalo is on its feet, but is disemboweled. Its sawdust-and-cotton innards are spilled upon the grass. Taggart, one of the medical students, holds a scalpel aloft in a gesture of triumph; several others dance around the body. The circle of dancers is broken by a trio of litter-bearers: Tiny Jim Atkins, head down, hands and feet dangling, is a difficult burden in spite of his size. Twice the litter-bearers try to hoist his limp body into the buffalo's open belly; now, on the third try, they succeed. One student squats on his hands and knees, bracing Tiny Jim's arched body with his back; a second arranges the ex-diver's buttocks and legs in the cavity formed by the buffalo's chest, securing him with heavy twine; the third completes the job aft, looping Tiny Jim neatly into the arch of the buffalo's belly, his head, neck and shoulders conforming to the swell of the animal's hindquarters, his eyes, nose and mouth visible in the generous slash from anus to genitals. Taggart stops dancing, puts his scalpel aside, and approaches.

"Very good, men," he says, and starts to sew the belly together with a long steel needle and stout surgical thread.

"Don't let them sew Jim up," the girl says to Peter. "You must do something."

"What?" he says. "What can I do?" Suddenly his stomach turns over and he staggers from the room and down the uncarpeted hall to the lavatory, and throws up. He returns, shaking, and falls back upon the bed, exhausted.

"Oh, Peter," the girl calls from the window, "they've finished. They've sewed little Jim up."

He tries to rise, but falls back upon the bed; she runs from the window to his side.

"You just can't leave him there," she says. "What kind of man are you, for the love of God? Jim is your friend. You just can't sew somebody into the guts of a water buffalo and *leave* him there. For the love of Heaven, do something or I'll go down myself and do it."

In a kind of frenzy she scrambles among the litter, retrieves her evening dress, and starts to pull it on over her head. Peter rises slowly.

"You'll be kicked out of school if they know you spent the night here."

He holds his head in his hands for a moment, and then reaches for the drink he has placed by the side of the bed. He takes a long swallow, puts the drink down, reaches for her hand, and drags her to his side.

"All right, all right," he says, "I'll see what I can do."

He rises wearily and gets a sweat suit, white wool socks, and a disreputable pair of tennis shoes from the closet, and slowly dresses. The girl is back at the window.

"Oh, it's awful," she keeps saying. "It's simply awful. Hurry, please, Peter, do hurry."

Outside, he blinks in the sunlight and holds his breath for a long moment, fighting the quick surge of nausea. The medical students have stopped dancing. A few are lying on their backs, half asleep; Taggart, who has put the finishing touches to the sewed-up belly, is sitting on the grass smoking, his hands clasped over his knees.

"Hi," he says as Peter passes by him, and waves his hand; ashes from his cigarette fall slowly to the ground.

"Hi," Peter replies and walks up to the hindquarters of the buffalo. Tiny Jim's eyes are closed, but his face, the little that Peter can see of it, is relaxed and happy-looking.

"Jim," Peter whispers softly. "Jim, can you hear me?"

Jim does not answer and Peter approaches closer until their faces are only inches apart. Jim is breathing like a baby, a baby with very strong, whiskey-tainted breath.

Peter reaches out his hands to stretch the aperture apart but Taggart approaches.

"I wouldn't do that, Pete," he says, his voice husky with alcohol and fatigue. "Leave Tiny Jim alone, will you? He's quite all right."

Peter brushes his hand aside.

"Jim," he says, "are you all right, do you want out?"

Jim says nothing but continues to snore, gently, ever so gently, like a baby filled with its mother's milk. Once again, Peter reaches forward to tear open the aperture but Taggart and three other medical students take his arms and push him away.

"I told you," Taggart says, his southwest voice only slightly menacing, "I told you, Pete, to leave Jim alone.

He's quite all right where he is. Now go on back to the room, Pete, and sleep it off."

What will I tell her? he thinks as he walks up the winding staircase. Outside his door he hesitates a long moment before knocking. At the sound, he hears her running from the window. When he enters, she puts her arms around his neck and kisses him, a long, affectionate kiss.

"He's all right, honey," he says. "Don't ask me why, but he's all right."

She says nothing but sits at his side by the bed and looks at him.

"Everything's okay," he says after a pause. "Leave him there, he's perfectly happy there."

He gets up and goes to his desk, and rummages around in the drawer. When he finds his Phi Beta Kappa key, he straightens up, closes the drawer, and returns to the bed. He puts the key in her hand and kisses her cheek.

"Don't worry," he says. He jerks his head towards the window. "They're about through, out there. When they all fall asleep or go to lunch, you can slip out. Everything will be all right. No one will ever know."

Goodnight, Ladies;
Goodnight, Sweet Ladies

❖ "Good God Almighty," Mercy groaned, and slammed on the brakes, hard, and slipped the convertible into neutral. We were driving very slowly, though, hardly moving, and weren't even shaken up. "I'm terribly sorry, professor," she said, "but I seem to have driven off the road or into a ditch or a tree or something."

She laughed a little, and cut off the ignition. She slipped over to me and put her arms around my neck and kissed me. She kissed me a long time, the way she had a couple of hours ago while I was playing the piano.

"You let me drive," I said after a while. "I think you'd better not drive any more. It's lucky we were going so slow. Christ, what a party."

It had all started out quietly enough. A cocktail party at the Paxtons', to use a euphemism. It seemed that every time I came back to Queensville someone was giving a party. Particularly the Paxtons. They were always giving parties. It made it nice for me. It had been pleasant to come back to Queensville every now and then, and to find someone from the old days giving a party. I'd been away from Queensville and the University for a long time. Not really away, of course. Washington was only about two hundred miles from Queensville, and I used to come back for a weekend every three or four months before I went into the army. Four years ago, that was, but it seemed longer than that. It was good to be out of the army. I'd been out a month. And it was good to come back to the University. The war had changed a lot of things. Even the University had changed. The School for Allied Military Government had just about taken over the place, and there were uniforms everywhere. Newly-commissioned American captains and majors with very shiny brass, occasional swarthy, stocky Filipinos, and here and there a Scots major in kilts and a little cap with two dark blue ribbons hanging down like a child's pigtails. Blue and white and tan-clad sections of briskly marching V-12's and Naval ROTC's had replaced the undergraduates in seersuckers and flannels and gabardines. The war had changed a lot of things, but it hadn't changed the quiet of the Lawn in late afternoon when the warm sun filtered lazily through the century-old elms and maples to cast mellow checkered patterns on the white-columned pavilions. It hadn't changed the feathery, pinkish puffs of the mimosa blossoms, or the haze enveloping the blue hills which rimmed the brick and columned world where I had spent so many good and bad years. It was good to be back. It was good to be looking forward to teaching again, even if I still was an instructor and might remain one the rest of my life. And it was always nice to go to a party at the Paxtons' again . . . .

There were plenty of drinks at the Paxtons' that night. There always were. Betty and Jim must have hoarded their ration coupons for weeks. Archibald, their houseboy, kept filling my glass with bourbon and branch water. Archibald knew me from the old days. He seemed glad to see me, back in a new seersucker suit. I was happy. Patton was sweeping unchecked through France, and Drew Pearson had predicted that it would all be over by the middle of September. No wonder everybody was happy.

It was getting stuffy and I needed air, so I elbowed my way through the crowd milling around in the drawing room. I stopped for a few minutes to talk to some people in the dining room, and to eat some shrimp. But my eyes were still smarting from the smoke, so I left the people clustered around the buffet, and limped through the kitchen and sat down at the top of the steps leading down into the pantry. I took a long drink of my bourbon and water, and lit a cigarette.

After a few minutes a woman sat down heavily on the step beside me. She was a small woman with a large bosom, and she wore a gray dress with small lemon-colored flowers splashed all over it. She had on a hat that looked like a mousetrap, and she reminded me of the pictures of clubwomen I used to see in the *New Yorker.*

"Give me a cigarette, young man," she said.

"Yes, mam," I said. "Do you like Players? They're very mild, but I like them." I gave her a Player.

"Thank ya'," she said, "thank ya' very much," and when she leaned over for me to light it I remembered her. Her husband was the Dean of Men. I had cordially disliked him during my undergraduate days. I felt a sudden flutter of anxiety. I had taught at American University before I went into the army, and I was still very nervous about deans and their wives. When I'm apprehensive I talk too much, and I began to talk too much then. The dean's wife sat and smoked and looked at my drink.

"I'm Peter Ross," I said. "I'm going to be in the English department this fall."

She didn't say anything, but sat sagging on the steps; after a couple of minutes the silence was becoming uncomfortable.

"I've just been kicked out of the army," I added.

"Oh?" she said. She had a soft, slurred voice. "Well, it's nice to have you back. May I sip your drink?"

I gave her a sip that turned into a slug. It seemed funny to be sitting on the pantry steps drinking with the wife of the man who had put me on probation years ago for cutting classes. That was the trouble, coming back to your old school where more often than not you'd made an ass of yourself. Everywhere I went I stepped on part of my past life. I'd be walking down the hushed Lawn at dusk in the soft violet haze and I'd turn a corner, and I'd stumble over a ghost from the past, a pale, slightly ridiculous ghost. Or I'd be sitting on a rock to rest my bad leg after driving to the dark green pine groves of Observatory Mountain when the thin fingers of morning mist trembled in the half light, and I'd remember a face, or a fragment from a forgotten conversation, and I'd turn to water inside. I'd limp past the Memorial Gymnasium and I'd think of the Finals dances there that had lasted till morning, or all the bad races I had run on that hard indoor track. I'd walk up Madison Road, past my old fraternity house where I had broken my wrist one Easter Week trying to jump from one balcony to another, and there'd be ghosts there, too, pale, ridiculous ghosts . . . . It was very bad, sometimes, coming back . . . .

The dean's wife had emptied my glass, so I got up and went into the kitchen. There were several bottles of whiskey on the sink and plenty of ice, so I mixed a couple of very strong drinks and went back and sat on the steps beside her. When she began to slop her drink over the gray dress with the small lemon-colored flowers, I realized for the first time that she was as drunk as a monkey, and I gave her another cigarette.

"I hear you've written a novel," she said. You couldn't tell from her voice that she was drunk, but her eyes were out of focus and her pupils were so dilated that just a tiny band of brown-flecked iris was visible. "Something about the world's end? I haven't read it myself. But I seem to 've heard Dean Throstle speak of it."

I was pleased that the dean's wife had heard about my novel. My first, and not a very good one, and probably my last. But the title was good. Trite but right.

This Is the Way the World Ends. A good title. Better than the book.

"It hasn't been published yet," I said. "Paper shortage. It may come out before Christmas, though."

"Good," she said. " 'm glad. Vurry glad. 'll read it. Like to read. Writing now?"

"No," I said. "I haven't had much time. But maybe I'll try to write a couple of short stories now I'm back here."

"Good," she said, and finished the last of her drink. Her blurred eyes suddenly snapped, and she smiled a big, pleasant, conspiratorial smile. "Look," she said. " 'll show you something. Unb'lievable. Exceeds your wildess' fancy. A profound secret. Incred'ble. 'll show you. You may write a story about it some time. A meemwah."

She gave me her hand, and I helped her to her feet. It was not easy. She was rocking on her heels, but she led me through the pantry and to a little closet where Archibald kept his mops and brooms. I was apprehensive, but I also wanted to know what this mild-looking, pleasant little drunk woman was up to. When she began to fumble with her dress I started to leave.

"Perhaps we'd better leave, mam," I said, and reached for her hand. "Perhaps we'd better go join the others."

She brushed my hand aside imperiously. "Doan' be an idjit," she said. "Doan' be an utter idjit. And stop calling me mam."

So she pulled up her skirt with one hand and pointed with the other, and there on the inside of her thigh were the faded blue tattooed letters V.M.I. The dean's wife laughed merrily and dropped her skirt.

"How do you like that?" she said. " 'Ginia Military Institute. Does that slay you, or doesn' it? You may write a meemwah about that sometime."

That was the kind of party it was turning into. Drinks from five-thirty to seven.

By nine o'clock everybody still at the party was feeling very good. The dean's wife and the dean and a lot of others had gone. I was standing in the middle of the drawing room. A lot of people were around me. Couples were standing in corners, smoking, waving their hands, talking quickly. I started to tell my favorite basic training story. By then I thought that everybody thought I was wonderful; this is a problem of mine. I felt like a Chagall lover floating over the Eiffel Tower. I got to the part about finding the fox in the foxhole when I felt two strong arms closing around my waist. They were strong arms, but they belonged to a woman because I could feel a woman's soft body against my back and legs, and then a woman's voice whispered *relax, relax.* Everybody was laughing; there was a blur of faces around us. What the hell is this, I thought.

Relax, the woman's intense voice whispered in my ear again; *relax, sweetheart.* Everybody was laughing and had crowded in around us. I thrust one of my arms out and felt someone grab the drink from my hand, and somehow I pulled off my glasses with the other and stuck them inside my coat pocket. *Relax, sweetheart,* the soft intense voice whispered again, and I felt the arms tighten and strain; the knees behind me gave a little, and then I was flipped through the air. I felt as though I'd been ejected from a missile. My God, my leg, I thought, but somehow I landed on my good one, and in a minute the room stopped spinning and everyone was laughing and clapping and talking.

I squinted through the haze of tobacco smoke in the general direction of the surprisingly small woman whose mighty arms had flipped me through the air. She had corn-colored hair and what looked like a bright, attractive fox-face. She was the wife of a Navy captain who was drinking straight bourbon in a corner of the room. His blouse was a mass of ribbons and he had a bemused, curious look on his face.

"You were wonderful," the small woman said. "I learned that in China," she said and started toward me with her arms outstretched, and I started to take off my glasses again, but her face suddenly went completely blank. Her knees buckled, and she started to fold up, slowly and very gracefully. Betty Paxton grabbed her before she hit the floor, and she and Jim Paxton carried her upstairs and laid her out on one of the twin beds in the guest room, and put some crushed ice in a towel over her forehead.

It was turning into that kind of party.

Everybody was having a good time. It was the sort of party where people drift in and out of your consciousness, wandering like ghosts in and out of the eddying clouds of blue smoke, talking intensely for a moment, and giving you a sip of their drink, and then vanishing. After a while I went into the music room to relax.

There was a crowd in there, but no one was at the piano, so I sat down and began to play. I really can't sing or play well, but sometimes when I'm terribly high I think I can. I thought I could play and sing that night, and everybody seemed to be having a good time. We sang "Someone's in the Kitchen with Dinah" and "God Bless America" and "St. James Infirmary" and a lot of others. Always there was the blur of faces and the insane drunken singing, and the confusion of people sitting on the piano bench beside me, talking or singing or falling off or giving me a drink or something. But then for a moment there was no more smoky blur, and no more hubbub, and it seemed as though the room were empty except for me and someone sitting beside me. Someone who took the cigarette from my lips and put her warm bare arms around my neck and kissed me lightly on the mouth.

"Hello, professor." The voice was soft and clear and cut through the smoke of the room, and it was as though bells were ringing on some high mountain place.

"You are wonderful with the Jasbo Brown routine, and I hear you were really gung ho with your daring young man on the flying trapeze act. What a time for me to be three hours late. I'm sorry I . . . ."

"Mercy," I cried, and my heart turned over and I tried to get to my feet, but she put her arms around my neck again and turned my face towards hers and kissed me. She kissed me a long time. It was as though I had never been kissed before. And then she got up and traced her fingers lightly over my forehead, and put a lighted cigarette in my mouth, and walked out of the room. Somebody gave me a drink, and I started playing the piano again.

I played the piano and I remembered Mercy, and I could still feel and taste her soft mouth. I remembered the first time I had seen her, and I wondered how I could ever have stopped thinking about someone I had once loved so deeply and then had hated so much. She had walked into A. J. Jackson's undergraduate class in Romantic poetry my last year in college. She was straight and fresh-looking and she had a head of hair that was like a flame and she wore a black raincoat and too much eye shadow. There were practically no coeds under fifty at the University in those days, and everybody stared at her, including A. J. Jackson. She seemed self-possessed but had difficulty finding a seat. She finally retreated a couple of steps and looked around and then some ape on the back row began tapping his feet ever so slightly, and then some others followed suit, and then some more. "That will be all, gentlemen," A. J. said, and the tapping subsided, but the girl in the black raincoat began to flush. The color rose slowly above the collar of her coat until her face was as red as her hair, and I guess I must have fallen in love with her at that moment. She never came back to that class, but I met her on the Lawn a few days later, and it began then. I became a mooncalf. All the poetry and all the fiction I'd been reading suddenly took on real meaning. When I saw her or thought of her, even in spite of the godawful eye shadow, I'd think of lines like "she walks in beauty like the night" or "clad in the beauty of a thousand stars" or "fair as a star when only one is shining in the sky." All that year she was the most important thing in my life until I found that while she had been reading poetry with me she was also sleeping with one of my best friends, slipping into his room on West Range at night, entering softly through the window and leaving an hour or two before dawn, and then the year came to an end, and I went home to Washington, and was tormented all that hot summer. And then weeks had grown into months, and I began doing other things, and then I had, or had I, forgotten her completely.

It was getting late. I stopped playing, and finished

my drink which had gone stale and had a few flecks of cigarette ashes in it. Everyone ran out of gas almost at the same time. I was playing "Goodnight, Ladies" when Mercy came back. She sat beside me at the piano. She looked as good to me as she had the day when she had walked into the Romantic poetry class. I finished playing and got to my feet. I felt Mercy looking at the bad leg, and turned away from her and started for the door. Everybody was saying goodbye to Betty and Jim Paxton who were staggering in and out of the front door with each departing guest. Mercy followed me into the warm, star-crazy August night, and took my arm, and steered me to her car. She started to help me in and I muttered, "None of that Catherine Barkley stuff, thanks," and got in somehow. She took the wheel and was doing fine, and then she drove the car into the ditch.

Fortunately we weren't going fast. She said nothing when I told her to let me drive, and in a little while I was able to ease the car back onto the road. I drove cautiously, and in a few minutes we were on Madison Road. It was after midnight and the quiet was like a benediction after the uproar at the Paxtons'. Mercy lived in the Monroe Apartments, high on Madison Road and overlooking Lawrence Field with its running track and playing fields bare and magical in the blue-gray starlight.

"Well done, good and faithful servant," she said when I finally stopped the car in front of the building. "Well done."

I started to walk away, but she took my hand. We entered quietly and somehow I made it up the stairs. Mercy dropped the key twice but finally got the door open. She switched on a shaded table lamp; white curtains fluttered in the night air, and the faint, clean smell of fresh flowers was everywhere.

"Tender is the night: John Keats," she said. I slumped onto the studio couch. Mercy stood by the empty fireplace and lit a cigarette. She was as beautiful as she'd been that first day in class. She walked over to me; she walked as well as she always had. She was a miracle to behold. She put her hands on my shoulders for just a moment, and then she turned around and walked into the kitchen. She came back and switched off the light, and the starlight flowed into the room like water. She went back into the kitchen, and I could hear her getting some ice and mixing some drinks. Then she was very quiet. Oh no, I thought, not that. My leg felt like kindling wood and I was completely dead. When Mercy came back, her bare feet made no noise, and her red hair was, like the man said, a cloud of fragrance on her white shoulders, and in the half-light her body looked as clean and fresh as a sonnet. She put the drinks down and sat beside me. I had a vision of the color rising in her cheeks as the ape on the back row began his gentle, insidious tapping, and I felt a wave of affection for her, but then, deliberately, I kicked over the drinks. Or was it deliberate? I didn't know, and I felt happy but I wanted out, both at the same time.

"I'm sorry about knocking over the drinks," I said. I took off my coat and put it over her shoulders. "You'll catch cold," I said, but it was warm and fragrant in the apartment. "I feel like a damned fool about all this," I said. I was suddenly no longer drunk, but very tired. "And I am sorry about spilling the whiskey."

I went into the kitchen, and mixed a couple of drinks, and took them back into the living room. Mercy said very little. She just sat and looked at me, and occasionally smiled a strange, curious smile. Something like the hallucinated look on the face of the captain who had been standing alone in a corner of the Paxtons' drawing room and drinking straight bourbon while his wife was flipping me through the air. Curious and understanding both. Or understanding and curious. But really more understanding than curious.

"I'll have to go now," I said, when I'd finished the drink. "And thanks for everything."

I took her hand. It was warm and somehow sweet, like herself. I said goodnight and started to limp across the room.

"You forgot something," she said. Her voice was very low. "You forgot your coat."

I turned around and started towards the couch, but she got up, swaying a little, and took off the coat. She handed it to me as though it were a death certificate.

"Thanks very much, " I said. "And thanks again for everything."

When I reached the door she was behind me.

"You son of a bitch," she said.

I turned around slowly. I felt terrible, but she put her hands on my shoulders again and kissed me lightly, not the way she had after I'd been playing the piano.

"You sweet son of a bitch," she said, and smiled.

I smiled back at her, and slipped out, and closed the door cautiously and limped down the stairs.

The Boy on the Bed

✤ Now that year David and his parents moved to the Southwest. His father hoped to be a novelist, not necessarily a very good one, and he taught at the University of Virginia, where the boy had been born almost seven years before; and his mother was consumptive, she had pains in her chest and spent half the nights coughing and chewing ice, until the darkness under her eyes deepened and deepened and she had to go to the hospital where they took many x-rays and then advised David's father to move his family to a warmer and drier climate.

It was a bad time for the boy, who came down with

51

the measles when they were half way across the country, near a place called Wichita. Even the soles of his feet were spotted, and he felt terrible for the whole week which they had to spend in a cheap hotel in Wichita. His father's groanings did not make David feel any better—"for God's sake, why does *he* have to get sick at a time like this"—until after they resumed their trip in their second-hand Ford and he finally saw a sign saying *Albuquerque, N. M.,* and his father shouted "New Mexico, here we are. Ahyahooooo!"

But things were not much better in Albuquerque where his father hoped to get a job at the University while his mother was getting better from the dry air. David did not like the high sky at first, and he felt embarrassed for the burned ground, so bare and bleached looking after the green trees and rolling meadows of the Virginia Piedmont, and he was overwhelmed by the huge mountains that rimmed the mesa, mountains like kneeling buffaloes shedding their hair, huge and wrinkled and foreboding. Sometimes in the early mornings the mountains were just a dark smudge on the edge of the western desert, but mostly they stood out so clear that David was sure he could detect the movement of animals along their scarred and pitted slopes. During most of the winter, after they had rented a pueblo-type of bungalow not far from the University, the mountains were festooned with wisps of white cloud in the morning and sparkled like jewels in the bright sun of midday.

David liked this. He was amazed and delighted that there would be snow on the mountains when it was so warm and sunny, and he liked to stand by the great cactus in their front yard and watch the bare-headed students drive by with skis strapped on the hoods and fenders of their cars.

Then his father got an advance on his novel and a job at the University, where he could work on his novel in peace and quiet, and they hired a maid named Virginia. She was from Texas. Negroes in Albuquerque were as rare as ticks on a hen's egg, and she was very black and beautiful, David thought. Every morning she came to work wearing a white uniform of some thin material that made her skin beneath it look blue, and when she walked she shook. David was fascinated by the way her front parts bounced back and forth as she ran lightly up the front walk, so different from the Virginia Negroes who always plodded slowly to the back door.

Sometimes David would pretend to lie dozing on the floor between the kitchen and the small dining room, and would look up Virginia's dress as she went about her chores, and once, when she leaned over the breakfast table to pour him some milk, he touched her front parts, and she shook her head and said, "What a naughty boy, I'll tell your mother if you do that again." And one night his father had to take his mother to the hospital and when Virginia came in to turn off the lights in his bedroom she put her hand, her warm black hand with the pink palm, under the coverlet and tickled him for a moment and he lay there rigid with delight and apprehension and then Virginia said, "Shush, David, and go to sleep and don't tell your Ma or she'll whip you."

He worried about this for some time.

Then his mother came back from the hospital and Virginia did not work for them any more and they had an Indian servant who was shapeless and smelled like

burning chicken feathers, and David grew even lone-
lier; there were very few children in the neighborhood
but only mostly old or sick people who had come there
to die, his mother said. He wrote a letter to his first
cousin Cecil, in Virginia, the only real playmate he had
ever had.

"Hello, Cecil," he printed the letter (he was proud
that he could write before most boys his age could even
read), "I wish i. could play with you I think Im a bit
homesick for you. Now I will tell you the Story of my
life. Once upon a time. as i was yong. But this is not
true I ran away and got. Lost and a giant ran. Out of
his den. Gobbled me up. And that was the end of me.
But then Virginia came and. Killed the giant. And out
i jumped of the giants belly and went home to play. My
My My My My I forgot i was in new mexico good by
Cecil my boy. I forgot abot. something. My address is
Las Lomas blvd. That is it, good by."

David was lonely all right, but it wasn't so bad as
long as his mother could play checkers or Parcheesi with
him, or just sit and chat, his mother dressed in a white
wrapper with pale blue or pale pink ribbons, lying on a
lounge in front of the big window and looking out over
and beyond the big cactus in the front yard, and he sitting or lying on the rug and drawing or looking at
books or making armies with his hands and fingers,
looping the second finger of each hand over the
knuckle of the index finger like the head of a horse
and galloping back and forth over the rug.

"It will be so good when you can go to school in the
summer," his mother said. "I know it's no fun for you
here, David, but in the summer you'll be seven and you
can go to school and you'll have lots of fun."

When his mother got sick again and had to go to the

hospital the smelly Indian woman left and Virginia came back to work, but she never let David lie on the floor and look up her dress and she never, no never, came to his bedroom and tickled him.

"I wish Cecil was here," he said one night at dinner.

"I wish he was too," his father said. "I know it's tough for you, David, with Mama at the hospital and me never home and so few children in the neighborhood. But in a little while you'll be seven and can go to school, and then everything will be fine and you'll like it here. I wish I could spend more time with you, but my novel, you know." He lay back in his chair and carefully massaged his forehead with his fingertips.

"When are we going back to Virginia?" David asked.

"I don't know."

"Is Mama any better?"

"Your mother is doing as well as can be expected," his father said. "Now don't trouble me any more, David. These are difficult times for all of us, and you must help just as much as you can. Now run along, like a good chap, and don't bother me any more."

David wanted to kiss his father, but his father seldom kissed him or asked him to sit on his lap, so he got up from the table and went to the front window and looked out at the great cactus.

The next morning was a bright Saturday, and after breakfast and three cups of steaming black coffee, strong enough to float an axe-head his father said, his father put down the morning paper and said, "Well, I see that they've opened the new library downtown; would you like to go see what it's like?"

They didn't get downtown often, what with his

mother sick and his father always rushing out of the house right after breakfast to get to work on the novel, and David's heart leaped with delight. Downtown was very different from the Northern Mesa where they and most of the other teachers at the University, slaves his father called them, lived. Downtown was the Santa Fe depot where fat Indian women in fancy blankets sold Kachina dolls and turquoise-and-silver jewelry and Indian pottery, and it was the dimly-lighted and smelling-of-leather museum with great curving steer horns over the doors and stuffed hawks and owls and coyotes. And best of all it was Old Town, where the hard-packed grayish earth had felt the heels and spurs of the Conquistadores centuries ago, with its sun-baked, tree-lined Plaza and canopied bandstand and ancient two-wheeled Spanish cannon and the twin spires of the Church of San Felipe de Neri and its shops and little theater and La Hacienda where at Christmas the trees were bedecked with wrinkled coneshaped red peppers and where from every gallery and balcony candles in sandfilled paper sacks beckoned in the darkness, and where David had seen an Indian he could not forget, with a coppery face adorned with straight black waist-long hair; in that face, in the eyes particularly, there was something that made David think of great distances and high windswept mesas and ceremonial dances and buffalo hunts and campfires under a star-crazy and limitless sky, and tom-toms throbbing like a pulse. And downtown was the city shopping district sliced right in half by the very East-West highway that had brought David and his family to New Mexico but which in Albuquerque was named Central Avenue, with its shops and hotels and movies and dark noisy places where in broad daylight a man had been shot and killed the very day after they arrived. "A great region, the Southwest," his father had said when he read about the shooting, "killings and saloons and whorehouses in the very center of town." And his mother had smiled and said, "Shush. David. Little pitchers have big ears."

So they went to the downtown library, which was a very handsome Spanish-mission type of building, his father informed him, the color of light yellow sand, with a bell tower and tall narrow windows and a pink-tiled roof and dark outjutting *vigas*. Inside, it was cool and airy and it had a special children's reading room with small comfortable chairs and low tables and a large tank filled with mysteriously bubbling pale green water in which darted many brightly colored fish, and here David felt really happy for the first time since the day he had come down with the measles on the trip from Virginia.

Almost every day thereafter, when he finished breakfast, he would walk to the bus stop on Central Avenue and ride downtown to the library.

At first he was happy just to sit in the children's reading room and browse through the picture books about New Mexico and the Southwest, books about the Spanish missions and Indian dances and the Conquistadores and the Rio Grande. He would wander through the open stacks, or sit and look at the fish in their green world, or gaze through the tall glassed windows where the sun cast arabesques through the branches of the poplars which were already in pale musky-looking leaf. Then he would go out into the warm daylight and sit beneath the trees and eat the lunch that Virginia had fixed for him the night before, and look at the cars driving west along Central Avenue, heading for the vast desert and Arizona and California, or going back east to the green land of high buildings and low skies.

He decided one day after lunch to do some exploring. He felt as free as a hawk as he crossed Central Avenue and passed the dark green bench where the bus stopped. He walked briskly towards an area of small shops; his heart was beating rapidly and he kept having to swallow as he remembered his promises to cross the Avenue only to catch the homebound bus. Angry and flushing, he retreated and fled across the street and back into the library where he plunked himself into a chair, which seemed much smaller than it had before, and looked scornfully at the fish until it was time to go home.

Each day, though, he would wander a little farther from the library.

Now it was the season of the spring dust storms and the usually crisp air, so dry you could wave your arm through it and hear it crackle, his father once said, was damp, and the mountains were blurred and shapeless. Farther from the library than he had ever been before, David could smell the dampness in the air as he stood by an arched and vaulted passageway, and peered at a narrow graveled path which twisted between a dark wall and a dimly-lighted bookstore. On a sudden impulse he stepped inside, took several squeaking steps, made a swift turn through throat-catching darkness, and stepped into a small plaza, a quadrangle vivid with grass and contrasting dark low shrubbery, in the center of which a fountain lazily spouted a stream of foaming water which fell splashing into a great bowl of smoke-colored pebbles.

Behind rows of dwarfed trees David saw low splashes of lavender, pale blue, lemon, and pink adobe buildings; approaching closer, he marveled at a law office which displayed a lifesized and bleeding Christus of painted wood; between it and the next room was an ivy-festooned recess within which the outstretched ceramic arms of a blue-gray St. Francis of Assisi formed a simple cross. A mural of galloping Indian ponies separated a doctor's office from a gift shop with its window alive with fiesta dresses, fantastically shaped glassware, and elaborately carved bulls, horses, and goats. The half-opened door of a real estate agency was illuminated with handpainted tiles; peering around it, David caught a disappointing glimpse of bare white walls, olive-green filing cabinets, and the inverted white-washed pear of an Indian fireplace. Suddenly he felt his skin crawl; was someone watching him? He waited, and looked around the courtyard. He saw no one. The plaza was empty and except for an occcasional muted rumble from Central Avenue was still as death.

As the rapid beating of his heart subsided, he tiptoed across the grass. Near the passageway, he noticed for the first time, were two smaller rooms which bore FOR RENT signs. David quickly scanned the empty plaza, and hesitated at the dark mouth of the passageway. After a long pause he returned to the first of the rooms and, straining on tiptoes, peered through the windows. The room was empty. At the door of the second, he hesitated. The greenish glass of its tiny window was elaborately framed in hammered silver, and was so clouded that he had to wipe it impatiently with his handkerchief. He pressed his nose against the glass and squinted through it. His heart lurched. The bare, clean room was empty except for a bed, a plain iron bed with a mattress, partially covered by a faded blanket, and in the middle of the bed lay a sleeping boy.

The boy on the bed was very beautiful.

He lay on his side, his face turned towards the door, the fingers of one pale hand dangling over the side of the bed like the petals of an inverted flower. His eyes were closed, with long lashes the same color as the dark hair which fell softly almost to his shoulders; he reminded David of the Little Lame Prince, so lonely and alone, although the Prince's hair had been honey-colored, and like the Prince he wore knee-length pants of some dark material and a jacket of the same color, and a shirt with a large collar like a bib. He had on white stockings and clumsy-looking high-quartered shoes, and David gasped again, this time in horror. Around one of the boy's legs, above the black shoe and below the white stocking, was a metal anklet of curious design, and to the anklet was attached a chain which was fastened to the foot of the bed.

Was the boy sleeping or could he be *dead?* He was so quiet. David shivered. This is awful, he thought, I want to go home. But the lonely figure held him spellbound, and courage slowly flowed again in his veins. David hesitated, raised his hand, let it drop, raised it again, and tapped gently on the clouded window. The boy did not stir. His hand still dangled over the side of the bed, and the dark lashes lay unfluttering on his cheek. David tapped on the window again, louder this time, and waited, his heart thumping. The boy's eyelids trembled, and slowly he opened his eyes and looked blankly at David. Then he sat upright in the bed, and in his eyes was a wide look of recognition, and he stretched out his arms towards David and opened his mouth and his lips implored "Help me, oh help me."

Behind him David heard the sudden crunch-crunch of heavy feet on the graveled path. He whirled around in panic. A tall booted figure towered above him in the grayness, and David fled across the courtyard into the dark passageway, through the curving corridor and out to the street.

It rained that night for the first time in weeks and David was feverish with plans to rescue the boy from his prison. In the morning he dressed impatiently, wolfed down his breakfast, and hurried to the bus stand. It was raining again and the mountains had disappeared behind sooty banks of cloud, and thunder rumbled in his ears as he made his way to the vaulted entrance of the passageway, slipped into the curving path by the bookstore and through the dark turn and into the courtyard, as beautiful as it had been the day before but different with the trees heavy with rain and the doves on St. Francis' outstretched arms dripping beads of moisture. At the heavy door with its hammered silver-framed window he hesitated for a moment; his eager breath clouded the window and he groaned impatiently. He peered through and gave a great cry. The room was empty, completely bare and empty.

He ran to the next room, and to all the others—the gift shop, the doctor's office, the lawyers' and the real estate agency—and back to the room and squinted with sick eyes into its emptiness. Then thunder exploded and the rain cascaded into the plaza; lightning flashed and a dwarf piñon tree sizzled and crackled, and David howled and fled to the street.

When he got off the bus and headed for Las Lomas Boulevard his wet clothes felt as though they weighed a ton. Water seeped through his sneakers and squished between his toes. He sat down on the curbing and thrust his feet into the swirling waters. The little boy is gone, he thought, killed, gobbled up, kidnapped, gone, and his heart felt as cold and damp as the rain. Two small girls emerged from a house across the street. "It's raining, it's pouring, the old man's snoring," they sang in high gleeful voices, and one of them waved a gaily-colored parasol at him, and called Hi, but he looked at her with silent contempt and turned his head away. I hope they catch a cold, he thought, and rose stiffly and splashed his way through the gutter, *idiots.*

Their house looked disreputable and tacky, the cactus sodden and dripping and rotten. He ran up the front walk and twisted the knob, but the door was locked, although he could hear his father's voice inside. He beat the door violently; then, grumbling and wetter than ever, he went around to the back. He kicked open the kitchen door and shook himself like a hound in front of the stove; it will do that nigger good to clean up the mess, he thought. He heard the front door open softly and he called out, pleased at the roughness in his voice:

"Virginia, come in here and clean up this mess!"

She did not answer. He stomped into the living room, grinding his muddy feet into the rug as hard as he could. Suddenly aware of his father in the hallway, he leaned down and fumbled with the matted strings of his shoes.

"What are you doing home at this hour?" David asked after a long pause, consciously imitating his mother's exaggerated Valley of Virginia reprimand.

"Didn't feel too good," his father replied, and pulled out a cigarette. He thoughtfully exhaled a long column of smoke. "And what, if I may ask, are you doing in this condition?"

His father extended his hand, hesitantly. His breath smelled bad, David thought, and he stepped back and looked at him, hard.

"I got wet," he said, finally; "I got wet going to the library."

His father looked puzzled, and David sidestepped him and went to his room and lay down. From his bed all he could see were the soaked skeletal forms of the tumbleweeds, and the drumming of the rain on the flat roof was like the twitching of an eye muscle when he had read too much. He lay on the bed and wished that he would never have to get up again. Later his father stood silently in the doorway and looked at him a long time without speaking. David wanted to run to him and throw his arms around him and cry out, "Oh Daddy the little boy is gone." But all he could hear was the drum-drum-drum of the rain, and all he could say was "I hate you, I hate you very much," as he turned his face to the wall and hoped that his father would leave him alone or go up to the University and peck away on his typewriter at a dirty novel that nobody would ever want to read.

The Gunner and the Apeman

✥ In the very center of the long elm and maple-bordered rectangle which is the courthouse square of Spottswood County stands the statue of a youthful officer splendid in the full-dress uniform and plumed cocked hat and high boots of the First Cavalry of Virginia. This is Major John Pelham, C.S.A., one of the most gifted of the soon-to-die officers of the Army of Northern Virginia early in the War when war meant adventure and glory and victory. In summer the loafers and the paregoric sippers and the scarlet-lipped girls from the wrong side of the river seek shelter from the white sun in the shade of heavy-leafed trees, and the statue casts a long shadow to the galleries of the pale

pink buildings that were old before Pelham was born.
But now it is winter and the trees are skeletons, and the
statue appears frozen in the light of a watery moon.

My friend the Gunner stands for a long time in front
of the statue, jingling some coins in his bruised hand
where the blood is drying in irregular scabrous patches
around the knuckles. In the thin moonlight the harsh
planes of his face are softened, and he looks, in spite of
what has recently happened in the hotel, incongruously
patrician. For a brief moment, standing there in the
moonlight at the feet of Pelham, he looks like the boy
he was when he played the part of General Washington
in the senior play when we were schoolmates before
another war, a boy who had two legs and could run the
hundred yard dash in less than ten seconds. Maybe it is
the high collar of the shapeless government-issue greatcoat or maybe it is the dark of the night, for the only
light comes from the moon, though if I look over my
shoulder I can see in the distance a few orange patches
of light which are windows in the William Byrd Hotel
where in a fifth-floor room a large man lies like a pile
of garbage in a bathtub half filled with icy water. .

The Gunner raises his hand and the coins ring like
bells when he drops them at Pelham's feet. He makes a
curious kind of half bow and then turns from the statue
and faces me. He is ready now for the long, limping
walk to "Cockroach Hill" and the seedy trailers where
the married students under Public Laws 346 and 16
live. He has been drunk three times tonight. Once on
whiskey. Once on violence. And now a third time on
something quite different. Something he may regret tomorrow but which tonight is somehow a river crossed, a
belief asserted, or simply an act of justifiable violence.

There is no violence here in this graveyard of the past with its pale buildings dreaming in the moonlight, its pyramids of cannonballs, and its quiet statues of warriors long dead. Their victory, surely, has been won. Maybe so with the Gunner, who was also a warrior, once. But now he does not care whether he has suffered another defeat or won a victory or been granted a meaningless reprieve.

We had stopped earlier that evening after taking a mid-semester exam, near another and very different statue, the kneeling figure of Homer, a blind man stretching forth his naked arms, hands uplifted as though in prayer, empty eyes staring at the circular library building which shines like a great red and white birthday cake at the end of the Lawn.

"I guess we busted that one," the Gunner says and fishes in the pocket of his recently dyed overcoat which is greenish in the lights from the white-columned red-brick buildings on either side of the grassy quadrangle.

"I guess so," I reply. I squint at the face of the great clock glowing on the pediment of the library.

"It was a freaking bad exam," he grunts. "I was crazy when I signed up for a philosophy course."

He rummages around in his pockets again.

"In nomine patris," he says. "Somewhere, aesthete, I have a piece of silver with which to propitiate the old boy."

He jerks his thumb in Homer's direction, draws a dime from his pocket with his other hand, and flips it at the base of the statue. He closes his eyes for a moment, and shoves his hands back into his pockets and limps towards the stone steps which lead to the lower range of colonnaded dormitories. He hesitates before turning slowly and looking at the statue.

"Wait a minute, aesthete," he says. "I'm going back to get the dime. I busted the freaking exam and besides I'm not superstitious." He limps back to the statue, grumbling. "Why I ever signed up for the philosophy of materialism . . . ? And besides I need the money to buy bread for my dear wife."

His voice trails away and then I hear him cursing.

"Can't find it," he says. "Let's go get a drink."

I feel around the frozen grass at the base of the statue.

"Forget it," he says after a while. "Let's go get a drink."

"It's after nine," I say, again looking at the clock on the library building.

"So?" he says.

"I told Mary I'd come home right after the exam. It's, well, it's sort of our anniversary."

"A fig for Mary," he says. "I should go home, too. I have only a dollar bill and a few dimes to my name and I should give them to my dear and pregnant wife. How much money do you have, aesthete?"

"About two dollars," I say. "But I should go home and study for another exam."

"Screw the exam," he says. "You'll bust it anyway, the way we did tonight. I should never have come back to school. Most of the professors here are jerks, as I see them. A malignant fate brought me back here . . . . My wife is bleeding and needs Vitamin K. But the freaking government has failed me again. My check is two weeks late, and I need money to buy vitamins for my wife . . . ."

"Okay, Gunner, okay, we'll go get a drink."

We walk slowly down the steps, and I shorten my stride so he can keep up with me: along the arched colonnades and by the boxwood gardens and through the massive gateway inscribed with the brave words of the University's founder: "For here we are not afraid to follow truth wherever it may lead."

As usual the Gunner halts beneath the arch where the Long Walk dribbles to a small triangle of concrete which is the stop for the downtown bus.

"Balls," he says, and crosses himself.

When the bus groans to a stop I take his elbow and help him up the steps. I drop our fares into the container and sit down beside him. It is a short trip downtown, beneath the C. and O. Overpass, by the Lewis and Clark statue with Sacajawea eternally pointing the way to new frontiers, past the antique and gift shops with their phony white pillars and fake galleries, into Vinegar Hill where in spite of the coldness knots of Negroes cluster in front of the fishfry joints and pool parlors and hamburger shacks, and finally we are in downtown Queensville. We get off at the William Byrd, cut across Main, and walk down Water Street which is gloomy even in the daylight and rank with the miasma which rises from the river. Pinpoints of light flicker through drawn cracked shades; above a closed door hangs an amateurishly lettered sign: AMVET's CLUB-HOUSE. I push open the door, we walk through a dark hallway and up a flight of creaking stairs and into a long bare room that always seems halfway dark in spite of the lights in the dirty walls and around the small bar.

"Our refuge," the Gunner mutters. "Our home away from home."

It isn't much of a clubhouse, but for students like the Gunner and me, to whom college means small government trailers on "Cockroach Hill" and pregnant headachy wives and not enough money, it is a refuge. Besides, you can't buy liquor by the drink legally in Queensville, but here you can get good enough bourbon and branch water for a quarter.

A few students like ourselves are talking quietly at rickety tables, but the room seems empty except for a big man I've never seen before. He looks out of place, in his fawn-colored, wide-brimmed Stetson and his light green gabardine suit with the wide lapels. He is waving a hand like a swiss steak in front of the bartender, a fighter pilot who is working on a master's degree in English.

"So I took the lousy bastard," the big man is saying in a voice like a cement mixer, "I took the black son of a bitch and threw him half way across the lobby of the Muehlebach Hotel."

He turns towards us as we approach.

"Ever been in the Muehlebach, son?"

The Gunner and I step up to the bar.

"No," I say. I drop a dollar bill on the wet surface. "Hi," I say to the bartender.

He mixes us some bourbon and water, and winks as he slides the drinks towards us.

"Thanks," the Gunner says.

"Ever been in the Muehlebach, sonny?" the big man demands. He has a massive flat ape face, with a nose like a baby's elbow and a weak Coleridge mouth that is

a terrible mistake. He wears a wide yellow tie deco-
rated with a villainous looking crimson trout. He pushes
up against the Gunner.

"Any of you freakin' rebels ever been in the Muehlebach? Best freakin' hotel in Kay See."

"No," the Gunner says. "No, and I've never been in
Kay See."

It is an insult the way he says it. He picks up his
drink and moves to the other end of the bar. I follow
him and lift my glass.

"Skoal," he says, and tosses off his drink. He slides his
glass down the bar and it stops directly in front of the
bartender. The bartender fills the glass with whiskey
and water and brings it to him and winks as the Gunner pulls out his dollar bill and slaps it down on the
damp surface.

"Skoal," the Gunner repeats, and drinks again, a little more slowly this time. I empty my glass and drop
two quarters on the bar. Just as I am picking up the refills, I see the big man's hand slap down on the Gunner's shoulder. Half of his drink sloshes onto his greatcoat and the color slowly drains out of his face. The big
man pulls out an embossed billfold from the inside
pocket of his slick gabardine suit and peels off a crisp
ten dollar bill.

"Hi, fellers," he says and smiles. "Let me buy you a
drink."

The Gunner picks up his glass and limps to the other
end of the bar.

"Excuse me," I say, and join him. His face looks like
last year's newspaper and the old tic has come back; the
lower corner of his mouth flickers like a horse wrin-
kling his hide to get rid of a fly.

"Take it easy, Gunner," I say in a low voice, and reach out my hand towards his shoulder, but he brushes me aside and beckons to the bartender.

"Who's the big YMCA man?" he asks in a voice like a cannonball in a rain barrel. "Who brought that big tub of guts in here?"

The bartender shrugs, and lowers his voice. "Never saw him before. Said he was in public relations."

"Oh no," the Gunner groans. "A freaking boy scout."

"Take it easy, Gunner," I say. "Take it easy, kid."

The bartender shoves two refills at us. "On the house," he says.

"Thanks," we say. I look at the Gunner and smile.

"Skoal," he says, and raises his glass. I relax and start to drink, but the big man pushes between us and almost knocks the glass out of my hand.

"Ya know, rebs, I once kicked the longest field goal ever kicked in Kansas."

The Gunner sets down his glass hard.

"Oh, Jesus," he groans. "A boy scout. A freaking boy scout."

The big man takes another step towards him. His big belly is about an inch away from the shapeless greatcoat.

"What did you say, son?" he asks. His wet mouth is twitching. There is a bewildered, piglike look in his eyes.

"Don't call me son, Jack," the Gunner says. I slide between him and the big man and hand him a cigarette. I take his arm and nudge him gently towards one of the tables. The bartender picks up a glass and assiduously starts polishing it.

"What's eating that bastard?" the big man asks. "What's he got a wild hair up his ass for?" Unsteadily he makes his way towards our table.

"What did you say, wise guy?" he asks.

"Get the hell out of here, big shot," the Gunner says. "Go off and kill yourself, Jack."

"Take it easy, Gunner," I say. I turn to the big man. "Look," I say. "Why don't you go off somewhere?"

He sits down between us, his belly bulging like a melon beneath the silky gabardine.

"Hey, bud," he bawls, "set us up here."

The bartender turns his back and goes to work on the glasses.

"Hey, bud," he repeats. "Snap outa it, bud. Some drinks for me and my pals."

"I'm not your pal, Jack," the Gunner says, and awkwardly starts to get up. With astonishing agility, the big man is on his feet. He catches the Gunner under the armpits and swings him from the floor. He holds him in the air a long second and then pushes him back into the rickety chair. It collapses and the Gunner makes an awkward attempt to recover his balance before he falls to the floor, one leg askew like a broken matchstick; I can see the olive-colored metal where his trouser leg has hiked up above his sock. Then things happen very quickly. I grab a piece of the broken chair and slam it down on the big man's baldspot, but it bounces off. He shakes his big head and grunts, and starts at me. I jump him. In spite of the big belly it is like hitting a rock. He makes no real effort to shake me off but just stands there and I feel like a monkey on a banana tree. The bartender helps the Gunner to his feet, and people crowd around us. Sheepishly I drop off the big man's back, feeling very much like a boy discovered stealing apples. The Gunner is standing on his good leg, shaking out the other gingerly. Our friends one by one go back to their tables or the bar; out of the corners of their eyes they look at the big man who is absentmindedly running his fingers through his thinning hair. Finally the bartender puts his hand on one of the massive shoulders.

"Get out and don't come back," he says. "Go back to Kansas City. Don't ever come back."

"Wait a minute," the Gunner is saying. "Wait a minute."

He approaches the big man, his right hand outstretched.

"Let bygones be bygones," he says. "Let me buy you a drink, mister."

He lays his remaining two quarters on the bar.

The big man grins like a child at a birthday party and shakes the Gunner's hand. He pushes the two quarters away and orders doubles for the three of us.

"I knew all along you were good Joes," he says. "I could tell you were good Joes the minute you come in."

What the hell's going on here? I ask myself, and look at the Gunner with a question, but he pretends he doesn't see me.

"Yeah, we're good Joes," he says.

"Married?"

We both nod.

He takes out the fancy wallet and riffles through the mass of membership cards until he comes to a snapshot in a plastic envelope.

"My dotter," he says. His voice trembles and his eyes

are suddenly wet with tears. I look at the snapshot of the big man half kneeling with a small girl sitting in the crook of his knee, a little girl in a frilly summery dress and the warm sun haloing her curly head.

"She's, uh, cute," I say after a pause.

"Thanks, pal," he says, and again his voice is husky. "Sweetest damn little ole dotter in the world."

He looks at the picture fondly before returning the bulging wallet to his pocket. The Gunner's eyes follow it like a retriever's. The man takes a great swallow from his glass, holds it in his mouth for a moment, and spits it upon the floor.

"Hawgwarsh," he says.

The Gunner turns to me. I don't like the look on his face.

"This is really a very nice guy," he says. "One of nature's noblemen."

The big man throws back his ape head and roars with laughter.

"My God, son, you're a comic, a real card." He pounds the bar in appreciation.

"This is an epiphany," I say to no one in particular. "An extremely revealing action. If only James Joyce were here now."

He looks at me quizzically, trying to focus his blurred eyes.

"Hawgwarsh," he says, wiping his eyes. He staggers slightly, steadying himself by gripping the Gunner's shoulder with his sausage fingers.

"Le'ss go to my hotel, sonny," he says. "I'll give you some whiskey worth drinking. Old Grandad." His eyes narrow; suddenly he is very crafty, very confidential. "Then maybe you boys can fix me up with a good lay."

"Sure, Jack," the Gunner says. "The night clerk's a good friend of ours. We'll fix you up with a good lay."

"I've got to go home," I say. "I have an exam tomorrow. And tonight's our . . . I told my wife I'd be home early."

"Chicken shit," the big man says. "What's the matter, sonny? Can't you get it any time . . . ?"

I take a step towards him but the Gunner's hand stops me.

"We'll go to the hotel and get our friend a good lay, aesthete," he says. Usually I wouldn't like the tone of his voice; it sounds like a skiff scraping against gravel.

"OK," I say after a pause. "We'll have a good drink of Old Grandad, and fix up our friend."

His eyes brighten. "I knew all along you were good Joes."

As we walk through the dark hallway, he begins singing a song about sunflowers. In the street he shakes us aside and squats like a quarterback, arms outstretched, his blurred eyes casing an imaginary enemy lineup.

"One—two—three, hike," he barks, and sprints crazily towards Main Street, his coattails floating like flags. By the time we get to the William Byrd, he is standing by the revolving door, his hands on the shoulder of a frightened middle-aged woman who is clutching a paper sack; apparently she has just returned from a late evening errand.

"If I had a face like yours, I'd wear a mask," he cries. "Brrrrrrrrrrrr!"

He covers his face with his hands and shudders, then throws back his great head and begins to bay like a coon dog.

"Good heavens," the lady groans, and scuttles back into the hotel.

I grab one of his arms and the Gunner takes the other. We shove him into the open wedge of the revolving door, and give a push. He is momentarily thrown off balance and beats against his glass prison with his tremendous fists. The door slows down, carrying him with it like a gargantuan squirrel. He beats his chest with one hand and pushes with the other.

"Wah-wah-wah!" he shouts. He is having the time of his life, and begins to dig in with his toes, like a sprinter coming out of his starting blocks. "Wah-wah-wah!"

As I push my way through the door next to the revolving cage, Billy the elevator boy and Harry Green hurry across the lobby. Harry is a good friend of mine. We were in basic training together and now he is going to the University during the day and night clerking at the Byrd.

"What in God's name . . . ?" he begins and then the big man spins out of his cage. He bowls over Harry and Billy as though they were infants. They sprawl on the floor of the deserted lobby, a tangle of legs and arms.

"Get up, mister," the Gunner says gently.

Tears of merriment stain the big man's red cheeks. "You're the best damned bunch of good Joes . . . ."

"Sure, mister, sure," the Gunner says. He helps him to his feet. "This is a good guy, Harry. We'll take your guest to his room."

Harry looks from me to the Gunner to the big man in bewilderment, and then back at me. I smile and make a circle with the thumb and forefinger of my hand.

"OK," he says dubiously. "OK, if you say so."

The Gunner and I lead the big man to the elevator. He is sweating like a horse. Billy is still shaky from his tumble in the lobby and the elevator rises in a series of jerks.

"For Christ's sake, nigger," the big man shouts. "Can't you run the freakin' elevator?"

He shoves Billy aside and begins fumbling with the control lever. The cab shudders and stops.

"Quit it, mister," I say, and his heavy muscles relax as I pull him aside. He throws his arm over my shoulder and I feel as though I'd been sandbagged. Now Billy has the elevator under control once more. We stop gently at the fifth floor and lead the big man down the hall. He has the best suite in the hotel, a lavender and old gold number with fake Matisses in the drawing room. He throws himself on the sofa and starts pulling off his shoes.

"Likker's in the can, boys," he says. "Go get it."

The Gunner is ahead of me.

"I'll get it," he says.

On the way to the bathroom he turns on the radio, and the midnight-till-one disc jockey blasts the air. The Gunner returns with a half empty fifth of Old Grandad and three glasses. He carefully pours the drinks, passes them and raises his hand. The big man half rises from the sofa.

"Skoal," the Gunner says, and swings the bottle expertly against the big man's temple. As the bottle descends a flicker of surprise wrinkles the big face; one massive hand claws at the air and fluttering incongruously pats and caresses the spot where the blow fell. He sits upright majestically, eyes staring at us in bewilderment. Then the pig eyes close, and spilled whiskey flows over his belly and down his legs. The Gunner drops his glass and the bottle, and slams his elbow into the big belly; the sounds of tearing cloth and a gentle sigh of pain are simultaneous. The big man collapses into the sofa; the sounds from his gaping mouth remind me of hog-slaughtering days back in West Plains when I was a boy. I turn my back and look out the window and force my drink down. Only then do I go back to the sofa and shake the Gunner's shoulder, gently.

"Quit now," I say.

He gets up slowly and rubs the bloody knuckles of his right hand.

"He'll be all right tomorrow," he says.

I don't look at the body on the couch, but go to the bathroom and dampen a washrag. After I wipe the blood from the Gunner's knuckles I mix him a drink and have another myself.

"Help me get his coat off," he says, a little later.

It is like pulling the clothes off a corpse, a warm, wet corpse. Then the Gunner methodically goes through the coat pockets. He takes out the fancy billfold, a gold pen, a leather case containing a nail file and comb, and a lot of keys in a leather holder. He flips open the wallet and thumbs through the plastic jackets with their membership cards and snapshots. He stops at the picture of the big man and the light-haired child with her hand on his knee.

"Sweetest little ole *dotter* in the world," he says.

Then he opens the wallet, takes out the bills, and counts them aloud.

"How much?" I ask.

"Three or four hundred," he says. "Got a knife?"

"A knife? No, I haven't got a knife."

He lays the bills carefully on the floor in front of him.

"Get a razor blade."

"A razor blade?"

"That's what I said, a razor blade."

"Where?"

"In the bathroom, probably. Look for one."

"What for? What do you . . . ?"

"Don't ask questions. Look for a razor blade."

I feel sick but go to the medicine chest. I come back with a blade and give it to him.

He slips it out of its waxy envelope, handling the blade gently and with respect, like a surgeon about to perform a difficult operation. He leans over the bed. The big man groans and his eyes flick open; he sighs and his eyes close. I go back to the window and pretend to look out over the darkened town. The Gunner hurries but remains calm. He slashes what is left of the green gabardine coat and hacks off the sleeves. From cuff to knee he slits the silky trousers and amputates the fancy tie.

Only then does he go to work on the money. From the thick wad he counts off the tens and twenties and very methodically shreds them to bits. When he accumulates a fistful he raises the window and slowly opens his hand. The breeze lifts the scraps in little eddies; a few fragments flutter back to the window sill, the rest slowly descend in the dark air. Then he closes the window and repeats the process until only a few singles are left. Very carefully he returns these to the embossed wallet and puts it back in what is left of the suitcoat.

He rubs his hand briskly together.

"Give me a hand," he says.

As we lean over the body on the sofa, the phone rings.

"What's going on up there?" Harry asks almost before I can get the phone off the cradle.

"Tell him everything's fine," the Gunner says. "No, let me speak to him. There's been a slight accident here, Harry. Yeah. Send Billy up in the service elevator in a few minutes, will you? And, Harry, better call a doctor after we leave. No, everything's fine."

Together we drag the big man to the bathroom. It is difficult but we manage to hoist him into the tub. The Gunner slaps his cheeks gently. His eyelids flutter and his hands make tentative pawing gestures. He slaps him slightly harder; color is returning to the gray face. Then the Gunner rises from the edge of the tub and looks at me and smiles.

"Let's go," he says.

He turns on the cold water faucet. The big man lies there like a vegetable garden in an August thunderstorm, what is left of his clothes darkening in the rising water. At the bathroom door the Gunner stops and clicks his heels together; then he returns and carefully raises one of the big man's eyelids. He nods, straightens up, and again clicks his heels.

"*Ave atque vale,* Jack," he says, and we walk out of the room and tiptoe down the hall.

Billy is waiting for us in the service elevator, the door open. Down in the basement he leads us carefully through the clutter of food crates, old chairs, broken tables, and miscellaneous junk. At the trucking entrance, he turns to us.

"Mr. Green, he says good luck," he whispers, and opens the door.

The cold air whipping through the alleyway is like a kiss.

"Tell Mr. Green thanks, and not to mention it," the Gunner replies.

We stop outside.

"Good night, gennelmun," Billy says.

"Goodnight, Billy."

We take a few steps, and the Gunner returns to the still-opened door where Billy stands watching us.

"And, Billy," he says. "Get back up there in a hurry."

"Yes-*suh*," Billy says.

We walk slowly through the alleyway. Ahead of us a rat scurries into a doorway, then turns around to regard us impassively. Beneath our feet the ground is gritty but the air is cold and fresh and I no longer think I am going to vomit. Then we are in the open and finally the courthouse square, pale and quiet, slumbers before us.

"It's been some night, hasn't it?" he asks me.

"Some night," I say. "How do you feel?"

"OK," he says. "I feel OK."

He pauses and shoves his hands into his sagging pockets.

"Wait there," he says. "I have something to do."

"All right," I say.

Slowly he limps across the cold grass. At the statue of Pelham he pauses. He says nothing for several minutes and then begins to fumble in the pocket of the shapeless greatcoat.

The Cross Country Dog

❧ "That was a tremendous story about Epictetus and his dog," I said. "It reminded me of another dog, a dog I hadn't thought of for years."

"Oh?" he said, and lighted a cigarette and fumbled with the ashtray on the dashboard of my car. It was a cold afternoon in early April, and he, a distinguished philosopher, had just completed a series of lectures on Ethics and Modern Man at the middlewestern university where I was an assistant professor of English.

"Would you like to hear it?" I asked. "It's on the long side, but the others won't be out to the club for at least half an hour."

He stretched his stocky legs and exhaled a great lungful of smoke. In his middle sixties, he seemed as vigorous as he'd been when I was one of his students at the University of Virginia. His thick red hair had turned a smoky gray, but his clipped moustache bristled as it had twenty years before, and his bright blue eyes were as fiercely inquisitive as ever.

"By all means tell it."

"It's really a very moral story."

"Good," he said. "Commence."

"All this began when I was coaching the cross country team at Virginia the last year of the war." I turned off tree-lined College Avenue and stopped at the traffic light.

"I was in Asia that year," he said. "I didn't know that you had been a coach. I remember that you ran when you were an undergraduate, but I didn't know that you had been a coach."

The light changed and I turned on to the blacktop road which wound its way to the country club.

"It was when the Navy had the V-12 program there," I said. "I just coached for a couple of years. I had a squad of about fifty men. Most of them were kids who'd enlisted fresh out of high school or with a couple of years of college. A few were older, about my own age a couple of them, and had been with the Fleet before the program took them."

"That was a good program, the V-12," he said.

"Most of them hadn't had too much experience. Or ability, either. But the Navy encouraged, you might say, their participation in intercollegiate athletics."

"Of course," he said.

"Their spirit was fine," I said, "but most of them didn't have too much talent. I enjoyed working with them, though. We used to warm up every day in front of Memorial Gymnasium. You know the reflection pool alongside Memorial Gym? It isn't there now, I understand. It's been drained, filled up, and grassed over."

He shuddered slightly. "I know all too well. A damned shame, if you ask me. The reflection pool was one of the most attractive spots on the Grounds. I remember once, years ago, I was walking home late one night, down the long flight of steps between West Range and the gymnasium. It was a black night, with a high wind. Suddenly a wild and terrible cry rose from the depths of the reflection pool. Curdled my blood. I never knew what caused it."

"The pool was full of fish in those days," I said. "Maybe a turtle or something of the sort."

He smiled at me indulgently. "Perhaps," he said after a pause, "though I never knew a turtle to shriek at midnight. But that's another story. Do go on with yours."

Beyond an elbow turn in the road I slowed down and stopped on the rough grass which sloped gradually down to the water hazard of the eighth hole; in the cool breeze the ruffled surface of the small lake was like broken slate.

"We're just a couple of minutes from the club," I said. "Shall we sit and look at the water for a bit?"

"Fine," he said, "but do get on with the story."

"Well, after they'd all warmed up, whenever we were running time trials—which was every two or three days, incidentally—the squad would start in front of the gym. They'd run one lap around the track . . . there was a cinder track, a quarter mile, around the reflection pool."

"I remember it well," he said.

"They'd take one lap around that track, head up the road that went past the New Dormitories, and finish up their three miles back at the gym. They always finished with that last lap around the track."

"Three miles," he groaned. "I couldn't *walk* three miles."

"Early in the season," I said, "there was a dog."

"Good," he said, "I was wondering about the dog."

"You know the kind of dogs that were always hanging around the University of Virginia?"

"Lord, yes. There never was a lecture at Cabell Hall that some dog didn't cause an uproar."

"Right," I said.

"There was never a football game at the University of Virginia, in all the years I've been there, that wasn't interrupted by some dog running onto the field and attacking one of the officials."

"That's right," I said. "But this wasn't that kind of dog. This dog was very shy. A medium-size dog. Mostly white, with a few tan spots here and there. There was some collie in him, I suspect, and maybe a little spaniel. Or some beagle perhaps. But this dog would never run onto the football field to attack an official. He used to hide in the boxwood."

"Hide in the boxwood?"

"Yes, you know, the boxwood in front of the gym. I think he'd been hiding there watching for days before I noticed him."

"That doesn't sound like a Charlottesville dog. I never knew a Charlottesville dog to hide in boxwood. Or anywhere else, for that matter."

"Well, this one did. I discovered him one afternoon

after the squad had started their time trial. I was sitting on the steps when I noticed this dog crouching behind the boxwood."

"What were you sitting there for? What kind of cross country coach were you? Didn't you ever run with the squad?"

"Oh, I'd run with them sometimes. But not every day. I was getting old. After all, I was twenty-five or twenty-six. I couldn't run *every* day."

"Oh," he said. "And the dog?"

"As I said, I noticed him crouching behind the boxwood. I just caught a sudden glimpse of his eyes, gleaming against the dark leaves. He was practically swallowed up in the foliage, and he had the saddest eyes in the world, that dog. Like a lion in a Rousseau jungle scene or something of the sort. But watching me intently."

"Watching *you?*"

"Yes. And not without some admiration, I think. He could tell I was the head man of that outfit."

"I remember a somewhat similar dog. Used to come into my introductory philosophy class, a most well-mannered dog."

"This dog seemed well-mannered, too. And so shy, hiding there and peering out through the boxwood. I immediately felt sorry for him. I spoke to him gently. I called him to come out from behind the boxwood."

"Did he?"

"No, but some of the fear seemed to leave his eyes. I spoke to him very gently. Then I had to leave, to time the runners as they came in. I timed each one of them, every day."

"Kept charts on them, that sort of thing?"

"Exactly. It's one of the few things a coach can do. Keep records. Compare their times. Get them to see they *can* improve."

"The dog?"

"For several days he was always behind the bushes watching the boys warm up. But he seemed more interested in listening to what I told them."

"That's interesting. What *did* you tell them?"

"Well, any kind of successful running is really more a matter of mind than body. You have to believe in yourself to be good at track or cross country. All the great runners have been tremendous egotists. Or neurotics, for that matter. No man can be a great runner if he isn't slightly neurotic."

"Like the dog?" he said.

"Exactly. That's why I became interested in him. He obviously had his problems, too. Gradually I started talking to him. Really talking, that is. Finally one day he came out of the boxwood. Followed me to the track where the boys were lining up for the start. That was some day, I tell you."

"Wonderful. He came out from behind the boxwood. You deserve a great deal of credit for that."

"Thanks very much. The boys deserve some credit too, though. They all helped the dog, too."

"The boys were interested in the dog?"

"Oh, extremely. I talked to them about the dog and his problems a couple of days after I first discovered him. I sort of thought I might make an example of him. Mind over matter, the will to win, that sort of thing."

"Very sound," he said. "Extremely sound."

"Each day I talked gently to the dog. It got so he left

his nest completely. He would be at the track each day, waiting for the boys to start running."

"Very good."

"The boys grew very fond of him. He became a mascot of sorts. Then I tried, ever so gradually, to get him to jog around the track with me. The boys liked this; this really tickled them."

"They were a credit to the Navy, those boys," he said warmly.

"Indeed they were," I replied. "A fine group. It was they who made the dog less fearful of things. He learned to like to jog around the track with them. But that's about as far as I could get with him. At least it seemed so at the time. He really seemed to be no athlete. He preferred to stand by and watch rather than participate."

"I've known dogs like that," he said. "The one in that introductory philosophy class was like that. As the bell rang he would walk in quietly, and lie down by my lectern. He never caused any trouble, but he definitely was lacking something."

A chill breeze rippled the gray surface of the lake, and we pulled up our coat collars.

"I think I remember that dog," I said. "But the cross country dog possessed prodigious hidden resources. It's too cold to stay out here any longer, though. Let's go to the club and have a drink before the others arrive."

"A good idea," he said enthusiastically. "But go on with the story while we're driving."

"Suddenly something seemed to catch fire in him," I said, as I started the car. "It can't be explained rationally, of course, but all at once he became engrossed with running. By the time of our first dual meet—with Gallaudet, the deaf-and-dumb college in Washington, you know—he would run lap after lap with any member of the squad."

"Wonderful."

"The day before the meet I took the Gallaudet team around the course. I ran with them, that is, to explain the course to them."

"I'm glad to hear that you finally did more than jog around the track with the dog. Do you always show the visiting team the course that way?"

"No, not always. But it's a nice thing to do. Particularly with a team like Gallaudet. The runners are all deaf and dumb, you know. And they'd never run in Charlottesville before. So I decided to run the course with them."

"Very good of you. Apparently you were becoming a credit to the coaching profession."

"Thanks," I said. "I'd just had a rubdown, and I was in the locker room, when the dog came in. Mouth open, eyes shining, twitching his hind quarters back and forth, wagging his tail, all that sort of thing. He put his paw on my knee and began to bark. There was some beagle in him, all right. What a bark he had!"

"A wonderful dog."

"I was thinking whether or not I could last the three miles, though. I'd been out late the night before. I almost ignored him."

"Poor little chap."

"Finally, I caught on. 'Do you want to run the course with us today?' I asked him. It sounds crazy, but his face brightened up like a Christmas tree. He was trembling like a racehorse. He leaped upon me, licking my hands in joy. Just then the Gallaudet coach came in to tell me his boys were ready."

"Wasn't he deaf and dumb?"

"Oh, no, not the coach."

"Did he want to run with you?"

"Not he, he was a fairly old man. Well, we started, the dog at my heels, and the Gallaudet team behind us. We jogged around the reflection pool and headed up the hill. Halfway up he began to whimper. I looked at him. He had a terrible look in his eyes. Looked as though he were drowning. A terrible look. Before we reached the top, he dropped out. Just quit and lay down in some bushes."

"Poor little chap."

"Yes, I felt bad about the whole business. I felt somehow he'd let the Navy down. Sounds silly, but that's the way I felt. I didn't enjoy the running at all. The dog, I hardly need say, was not at the track when we got back."

"Was he hiding in the boxwood?"

"No, he wasn't there, either. Nor the day of the meet, which we won, incidentally."

"Good going."

"Yes," I said, "it was nice to begin the season with a victory, even against a small school like Gallaudet. All of us felt pretty bad, though. The dog seemed to have disappeared. Somehow it took the zing out of things for a while. I had a morale problem with the team, I can assure you."

I turned onto a graveled road lined with enormous elm trees; by midsummer the road would be arched in a fretwork of lacy green, but in this cold spring only the tips of the upper branches showed a slight dusty fuzz. We parked and entered the low white building.

"How about that drink?" I asked.

He rubbed his hands together and smiled. The club

was empty, except for the bartender, and we sat down in the corner I always liked, overlooking the surprisingly green golf course, its rolling fairways reminiscent of some of the cross country courses I had run years before. The bartender brought us our drinks and we clinked glasses and waited for the dinner guests to arrive.

"That's a good story," he said, "but a sad one."

"I haven't finished yet," I said, and took another long swallow. "I was faced, as I said, with a serious morale problem. We were all off form for several days. And we were badly beaten in our next meet. With the Naval Academy. Nobody ever beats Navy in cross country at Annapolis, of course, but we were really awful."

"You did have a problem, no doubt about it."

"The Monday after the Navy meet I was sitting on the steps of the gym before practice. I heard something behind me, a kind of groan, and realized immediately that the dog had returned."

"He was hiding in the boxwood again?"

"Exactly."

"Poor chap."

"That's exactly the way I felt. I was delighted to see him, though. But his eyes were as sad as they'd been the first time. I spoke gently to him, but I couldn't coax him out."

"The same problem all over again?"

"Precisely. I told the squad about him, of course."

"How did they react?"

"They were delighted. Several of them came to talk to him, but all he did was shrink deeper into the boxwood."

"This is becoming a heart-rending story," he said,

and finished his drink. "And I'm sure you're exaggerating."

"Every word is true," I protested. "But it has a kind of happy ending. Almost. In a way, that is."

I signaled the bartender for more drinks, and lighted a cigarette.

"I'm glad of that," he said. "Go on."

"I sent the boys off on their workout. They did well that day, even the poorer members of the squad."

"Good."

"On my way home," I said, "I stopped in front of the gym. The poor devil was still there, cringing in the boxwood. I picked him up and carried him home. I lived on Lewis Mountain Road that year. Just a short walk from the gym."

"Yes, I know Lewis Mountain Road well."

"I heated some milk, and gave him some cereal in a bowl. After he ate, he came and lay at my feet. I talked to him for some time, and he seemed to be feeling better."

I regarded my friend carefully. He had a faraway look in his eyes and was gazing over the rolling fairways.

"I'm not boring you, am I?"

"Of course not," he said. "It's a most impressive story."

"I'll have to compress it," I said. "The others will be getting here soon. To make a long story short, the dog became completely rehabilitated. As in the past, he'd be waiting for me at the track every day. Finally, at our last big time trial before the Southern Conference Meet, he again came to the locker room."

"Mouth open, eyes shining, wagging his tail, and all that?"

"Exactly," I answered. "I knew, immediately, that he was ready to go the distance. I hadn't planned to work out with the squad that day, but decided to make the sacrifice. It was one of those magnificent November days in Albemarle County when the air is so bright it hurts and you can almost feel it crackle. I was just about as excited as the dog."

"Most beautiful county in America, Albemarle," he said.

"Well, I got suited up, and had a rubdown, and we all lined up at the start. The whole squad, about fifty of them, eager and ready, and myself, and the dog. We took off around the reflection pool, running easily, all bunched together, feeling wonderful. But halfway up the hill, I could sense the dog's fear returning. I could almost feel him shudder . . . . He was right at my heels, you understand."

"That dreadful hill," he said sympathetically. "The moment of truth."

"Exactly," I said. "I leaned over and rubbed his ears, and gave him a little pat on the rump. He looked up at me, and the fear seemed to fade from his eyes. He stayed with me, and I went up the hill faster than I'd done all season. By the time we'd passed the Engineering Building only my captain, a wonderful runner named Joe (he was a Southern Conference distance champion the following year), only Joe and three or four of my best men were still running close to us. The rest were stringing out behind, as they always did after the first half mile or so, and the dog was trotting along almost without effort. He had a grin from ear to ear, and I leaned over and patted him again."

"Wonderful!" he said.

"By God, it *was* wonderful. At the halfway mark—by

that winding dirt road that branches off to Observatory Mountain—Joe, the one I said was a Southern Conference champion, began to lengthen his stride. 'Kick it on in, Joe,' I called as he passed me. The dog seemed to hesitate for a minute, and looked at me out of the corner of his eye. 'Give 'em hell, boy,' I said, and leaned over again—I was wearing myself out doing this, you understand—and patted him. He looked at me again and flicked his tail, and was off like a flash."

"Bravo!" The bartender had refilled our glasses, and I paused as a group of middle-aged ladies filtered through the lounge in a miasma of powder and cigarette smoke, and noisily decided it would be Bloody Marys rather than Old Fashioneds.

"I really felt good at that moment," I said. "Most of the rest of the course is downhill, and the last mile circles around the New Dormitories. You have an almost unobstructed view of the Gymnasium and the reflection pool. Two or three of my boys were passing me at about this time, but I could see Joe and the dog hit the far end of the track simultaneously. They were running stride for stride. Neck and neck, or paw to toe, you might say."

"Very good," he murmured.

"As I headed for the pool, the dog went into the lead. He was about five feet ahead of Joe. But then Joe uncorked the best finish he'd run all year. I think he must have run that last quarter mile in about fifty-five seconds. That was phenomenal in those days. But the dog stayed in front all the way."

"Good show."

"I lost sight of him for a little bit," I said. "Several of the other runners passed me on the track. I was pooped out, I can tell you. But what do you think I saw when I'd finished?"

"I have no idea. What *did* you see?"

"By Heaven, the dog was still running. Around and around the track. Having the time of his life, he was."

"What a wonderful dog. And a wonderful story, too."

"Many thanks. The other runners began to come in, by two's and three's. The dog continued running. I began to get worried. I tried to catch him once as he came down the straightaway, but he sidestepped me. He just kept jogging around with each man as he came in. Always kept a few feet ahead of each finisher. Until the cellar squad, that is."

"The cellar squad?"

"Five or six who always came in last. Nice lads, good officer material, but simply no aptitude for running."

"I see."

"When the cellar squad staggered around the far curve, the dog slowed down. On the back stretch he turned and barked at them encouragingly. As they weaved into the final straightaway, he was scarcely moving."

"Just kept the same distance ahead of them, eh?"

"Precisely. Until the finish, anyway."

"Until the finish? What happened at the finish?"

"What greatness that dog had in him! A few strides from the finish he slowed down to a walk. Let every last man on the cellar squad pass him."

"Marvelous. *Le moment suprême!* Absolutely marvelous!"

"I tell you, it was one of the greatest days of my life. The entire squad had assembled at the finish line

When the last man was in, there arose one of the greatest cheers I've ever heard in my life. We all rushed over to congratulate the dog, but . . . ." I paused and took a sip of my drink.

"But what?" he smiled. "But me no buts."

"As the last man staggered off the track, the dog gave a tremendous bark. He looked at me proudly, and side-stepped me again. Then he took off around the track like a ball of fire. I was too excited to time him, but I know it's the fastest that track has ever been run in, before or since. He started off like a sprinter, high on the balls of his feet, his tail straight behind him like an arrow. He was a blur coming down the stretch and exploded, simply exploded, across the finish line. As he slowed down, we all cheered again. He was wobbling, but he turned around and looked at us, and grinned. He'd really had it physically. He was as lathered up as a racehorse, and his tongue looked like a rope, but he was exultant."

"A wonderful story," my friend said. "And, as you mentioned, a very moral one. *Ad astra per aspera.* Or *Pluck and Luck.*"

"Not quite," I said. "Alas, not quite. Do you know the William Steig drawing, 'Glory?' A naked man holding aloft another man's severed head? Wearing the greatest victory look in all history? The man holding the head, that is. Well, the dog looked at me like that for a split second. A look of triumph. But also a wild look. I didn't like it. A kind of crazy glare, like the animals in a horror movie."

"Come, come, Bill," he said.

"It's a fact," I said, and paused. "Do you remember the story you once told me of the mad surgeon who performed a delicate operation in a vast amphitheatre while specialists from all over the world watched spellbound for three hours? And burst into applause at the successful conclusion?"

He thought for a moment. "Yes, of course," he said, finally, and his ruddy face lit up with a smile. "And when the applause dies down, the surgeon bows, picks up a fresh scalpel, and commences to amputate his own leg as an encore."

"Exactly," I said. "Similarly the dog. He stood there and looked at me for a split second. He was drunk . . . ."

"Your guests are here," the bartender leaned over and told me. I made the introductions, and we chatted for a while over drinks and went in to dinner. Later, driving back to town, my friend was silent. As we approached the hotel where he was staying, he turned towards me.

"All right, Bill," he said, "Don't hold out on me."

"Hold out on you?"

"The dog," he said. "He was standing there looking at you."

"Oh," I said. "The dog. You really like the story, after all. He was drunk with fatigue and glory. But he hadn't had quite enough. He wasn't completely satisfied. Just one split second he stood there, weaving, with that wild triumph in his eyes."

"And then?"

"He gathered all his resources for one last mighty effort. He gave a great bark, took a couple of faltering steps, and jumped—or, rather, sprang—into the reflection pool."

"Jumped into the reflection pool. Good Heavens!"

I parked the car in front of the hotel.

"I know you must be tired," I said. "Your lectures have been marvelous. I'll pick you up in the morning and drive you to the airport."

"The reflection pool," I heard him mutter as he got out of the car. "The reflection pool. Good God."

At the revolving door he hesitated a moment, and turned around.

"Poor little chap," he said. "And then what happened? After he jumped. Tell me you fished him out. Don't tell me that he drowned."

"But that's another story," I said, and waved, and drove away.

The White Shell Road

✤ The cold water felt good on his back and shoulders and for the first time in many months he broke spontaneously into one of the old songs from his undergraduate days, something about Rugby Road and Vinegar Hill and loving cups and drinking toasts. Afterwards, he dried himself meticulously and combed his hair and rested on the seat of the toilet. He smoked in silence, savoring the scent and taste of the tobacco; then, barefooted, he tiptoed into the bedroom. Helena was still asleep, so he slipped on his dark blue dressing gown and sat down by the side of the bed. He reached for the tumbler on the bed table, but the ice had melted and the remains of his drink were flecked with cigarette ashes. He walked quietly into the small sitting room to mix himself a highball; there was still plenty of ice in the plastic bucket and the bourbon was fresh and clean tasting.

He stretched his legs and relaxed, and gazed at the picture on the opposite wall, typical grade-A hotel art. Typical, that is, except for the white shell road in the foreground. Beneath a hot summer sun the road meandered white and blazing to an unseen shore where he could envision blue-green tidewater ceaselessly eating upon an unresisting body of white sand. The picture had impressed him, and disturbed him; it was the first thing he had noticed when he and Helena checked in the night before. He had known shell roads like that in his boyhood, many of them. They reminded him of summer days, girls lithe and lovely in fresh-smelling dresses and tree-shaded lawns and cool summer nights with clouds of fireflies floating in lavender mist, of Fourth of July concerts and fireworks after the races and the warm smell of salt drifting up from the bay. Above all, the road reminded him of Helena.

He tiptoed back into the bedroom and picked up the copy of Ernest Dowson's poems, an inexpensive imitation leather edition he had given Helena several years ago, back before his marriage, when he still had hopes of teaching her to read poetry, even bad poetry. Almost automatically the book opened to "Cynara"; he laughed without humor when he came to *Yea, I was desolate and bowed my head,* which she had underlined in pencil. He closed the book and finished his drink and studied Helena's flushed face; for the life of him, during the months and years since they had been lovers, he could never really visualize her, could never remember what she really looked like, even though he had known her since she was a skinny, long-legged runt with straw-colored hair who always won the fifty-yard free-style in the club contests. She was prettier than he had remembered, beautiful actually, except for her teeth which were slightly protruding; she had probably been a thumbsucker, he thought, thinking of his own three-year old son.

Why do I love her so when she's asleep? He started to trace the light blue veins of her closed eyelids, and thought of Keats' lines about Madeline in "The Eve of St. Agnes": *and still she slept an azure-lidded sleep, in blanchèd linen smooth and lavendered.* He had once asked one of his students what the lines meant and she had said she didn't know but maybe they meant that Madeline was wearing eye shadow or something. Helena wasn't that dumb, he thought, and withdrew his hand and started to return to the sitting room to get another drink, but stopped at the sight of her rosy sleeping face, so childlike yet at the same time so ravaged. Why do I love her so when she's asleep, he thought again, and yet get so bored with her when she's awake? Again he leaned over and picked up her left hand and ran his fingers lightly over the imitation silver band which they had bought the night before. She sighed and pressed his hand, and then very suddenly she opened her eyes and sat up.

"Darling," she said, and stretched her arms towards him.

He sat down on the side of the bed and placed one arm around her shoulder and stroked her hair gently.

"I adore you," she said. "You are my life, really."

"You shouldn't say that," he said after a pause. "I

don't know what to say when you say things like that."

She sighed, and turned over and half buried her face in the pillow.

"I shall be in prison when you're gone," she said.

"Don't talk like that," he said. "Or talk about it if you must, but don't think like that. Prisons are no worse than deserts. For Christ's sake, don't talk like that."

She turned over, the tears springing to her eyes as though he had struck her on the mouth.

"I'm sorry, Helena," he said. "You know I'm sorry. But you mustn't talk like that, really, for your sake or for mine."

He took her hands and kissed them and, again, stroked her forehead with his fingertips.

"It's a bad business," he said. "It was a mistake, I guess, this."

"No, no!" she said. "It was not a mistake. I'm foolish, that's all. I do love you so, and I can't bear the thought of not seeing you."

He withdrew his hand and went into the sitting room. He took a long time mixing her drink and scrutinizing the white shell road in the painting, the road, he suddenly recalled although he had not thought of it for many years, that led to the bay at Blue Island, and the old hotel, and the marvelous fountain. He hastened back to the bedroom and gave her her drink; her eyes were the color of the water in the fountain, sometimes blue, sometimes green, and always suggesting a depth which he knew did not really exist.

"You remember Blue Island, don't you?" he asked as she sipped her drink gratefully. "The picture,"—he jerked his thumb towards the sitting room—"it reminds me of it. There was a road there like the one in the picture. When I was a boy. A white shell road. Of clam shells, and they seemed white and blueish or pale pink in the sun, but gray and dead-looking in the winter. There was a road like that, just like it, from the hotel we used to stay at. It went from the hotel almost down to the beach. About a mile. You remember Blue Island, don't you?"

"Sure," she said. "We went there for a couple of summers, too. It was old fashioned then, though. It was dull. The water was good, though."

"It wasn't dull when I was there."

"There was a houseboat where you could get wonderful softshell crabs."

"I remember that," he said. "We went there a lot."

"The hotel was getting run down then. And I don't remember the white shell road. I remember a lot of old men and women who sat around on the porch all the time. I didn't like it there. It was dull."

"It didn't seem dull to me," he said. "But that was a few years before you were there. It was getting run down, though, I admit. But I loved that road. You wouldn't have known you were near the water, just dry fields, except that you could always smell the salt. Then all of a sudden the road ended and there was the beach."

"They had a good diving board," she said. "I learned to do a gainer on that board."

"What I liked best was the fountain in front of the hotel. It was the most wonderful fountain. That's what the road really reminded me of. I loved that fountain. I used to spend a lot of time just looking into it."

"Dull," she said.

"No, it wasn't dull. And during the winters, I'd count the months and days till we'd go back to Blue Island again. It had turtles and fish in it. It looked about a mile and a half deep. The water was dark and green and well, pretty damned wonderful."

"Ummmmmm," she said.

"It was like your eyes."

"Good," she said, and stretched out her hand. He held it for a moment, then let it drop back upon the bed.

"It was really wonderful," he said. "I went back there, a few years ago. I hadn't been there for years. I wanted to see the fountain."

"Did you get any softshell crabs?" she asked.

"It was winter when I went back. The houseboat was closed."

"What about the hotel?"

"It was closed too. It'd been closed for years, I guess. It was falling apart. There were no old men and women sitting on the veranda."

"Too bad," she said.

"Too bad, for Christ's sake! It was terrible!"

She closed her eyes and looked absently at the ceiling.

"Give me a cigarette, darling; I'm dying for a cigarette."

He fumbled absentmindedly in his pocket and withdrew a cigarette; he put it between her parted lips and tossed her a pack of matches. She opened her eyes and looked at him narrowly.

"Aren't you going to light it for me?"

"Oh, for Christ's sake . . . all right, Helena, here."

She smoked slowly in the silence.

"Oh, darling," she said. "Don't be unreasonable. I'm just on edge. I'll be miserable without you."

"Don't think about it," he said. "I'm sorry. Let me tell you about the fountain."

"Oh, damn the fountain; let's go back to bed."

"Okay, okay, if you feel that way, let's go back to bed."

She sat up, her green eyes blazing, and he turned his head from her.

"Why must you be like this?" she asked. "Why must you be like this, tonight of all nights in the year?"

"Don't talk like that," he said. "Why do you have to keep quoting that phony Poe all the time?"

"Poe?" she asked. "Who's quoting Poe?"

"Forget it," he said. "I'm sorry, Helena. Forgive me."

"Tell me that you love me," she said after a pause. "Just this once, tell me that you love me."

"I can't say that," he said. "You know I can't say that."

He reached out to touch her, but she rose quickly from the bed and walked stiffly into the bathroom. Then, in a few moments, he heard her singing in the hissing shower, and he smiled and lay down on the bed and closed his eyes. Her kiss, light and cool, awakened him.

"You *are* sweet, Helena," he said and put his arms around her.

"How nice you can be," she said. "I do adore you, and I'll never say again that I cannot live without you."

She lay beside him quietly, one warm arm around him.

"Tell me about the fountain," she said.

"The fountain? Oh, there's not much to say about it, really. I just went back there that winter I was telling you about. It was all dried up, of course. There was no water in it. No fish or turtles. It wasn't nearly as deep as I'd remembered it."

"Too bad."

"Instead of the fish and the turtles there were a lot of cigarette stubs, and candy wrappers, and used condoms."

"How horrid."

"That's the way it goes," he said. "You win a few, you lose a few."

"How true," she said. "Trite but right, as you used to say."

"Ouch," he said, and leaned over and kissed her eyelids.

"You look like a child," he said.

She smiled at him.

"Oh dear, I'm so sorry. I don't feel like a child."

"Or a nun." He glanced at her dress, thrown carelessly over a chair. "Or at least you did, in that dark dress. And with those lovely dark bags under your eyes."

"I almost thought of being a nun," she said. "Remember?"

"Yes," he said, "I remember. But now you're a nurse. A good one. And you're going away . . . ."

"Oh, don't say it," she cried. "I can't bear it."

She put her arms around him and hugged him as if he were a doll.

"How much time do we have?"

He looked at his watch.

"It's seven-thirty," he said, "and your plane doesn't leave till midnight. We have lots of time. We should get some food, though. You need the food. You haven't eaten decently since we got here."

"I don't want any food."

"Why won't you eat?" he persisted. "For Pete's sake, why won't you eat?"

"I don't want to eat. I can eat alone for the next fifty years. I'm so hungry I'm weak, but I can't eat."

He reached out and patted her hand.

"Please," he said.

"No," she said.

"Let's go for a walk, then. Let's get up and go for a walk."

All through the day and afternoon the rain had fallen dully, but now a thin moon rose above the glowing buildings, and the washed city was sleek and shining. The air was fresh and clean smelling, and he impatiently threw away the cigarette he had just lighted. They walked aimlessly, and she put her hand in his, and traced her fingers against his palm. He wanted to kiss her and tell her he was sorry, and hold her in his arms. Just hold her in his arms and touch her breasts gently, and feel her against him and remember what the night and day had been like, and the quiet rain and the food she hadn't been able to eat and the increasing uneasiness in his innards as the hours floated away like the ragged wisps of clouds and every minute was that much closer to midnight. Then he heard the sudden grinding of brakes and a high scream of pain. He had heard men scream like that, when the flesh was torn and the bones were broken and the soul was suddenly jolted loose from the body.

"Mother of God," Helena cried. "What was that?"

A small crowd had already gathered at the corner where a smallish woman in a light gray coat was leaning over the twitching body of a honey-colored spaniel, and the cab driver, fumbling with his cap, was standing by his cab.

"Dear little fellow," the woman was sobbing as she knelt over the dog. "Dear little fellow."

She stopped and gently picked up the broken body, the useless leash dangling from his collar. She cradled him against her breast like an infant. The dog had stopped screaming and lay panting in the woman's arms, his tongue trembling, his eyes bulging. Blood and slime streamed from the dog's hind quarters; the woman's gray coat was stained with his destruction. The dog coughed, its dangling hind legs twitching like a frog's just severed from the torso; he snuggled against the gray coat and coughed, and the blood streamed from his gaping mouth.

"Dear little fellow," the woman kept repeating. She cried, not wildly, unrestrainedly. She stroked the dog's head.

"Poor little head," she said softly.

He grasped Helena's arm and pushed her through the already dispersing knot of bystanders. The air was suddenly close and he was uncomfortably conscious of the smell of his own body.

Back in the bedroom, Helena waited for him quietly while he poured a drink, but all the ice had melted and the whiskey tasted foul.

"The poor woman," Helena said.

"Yes," he said.

He sat down beside her and she set the alarm and switched off the light.

"I have something for you," she said later.

"What is it?" he asked and then the hard circle, still warm from her finger, was in his hand.

"Don't you want it?" he asked.

"Not any more," she said. "Not now. And I have no use for it where I'm going."

"Are you sure?"

"I think so."

"But are you really sure?"

"Yes, I think so."

"All right," he said.

"I guess this is it."

"Yes, I guess so."

"Are you glad?"

"No," he said. "Of course, I'm not glad."

"Will you think of me?" she asked.

"Of course," he said. "Constantly."

When he returned from the airport he walked around the block two or three times before going back to the hotel. In the bedroom, he took off his coat and carefully hung it in the closet. He poured himself a drink and loosened his tie. The scent of her was still in the bed, and he avoided brushing against the rumpled sheets. He skirted the bed warily, like a boxer feinting to feel out an opponent's weakness. He went into the bathroom. Helena had forgotten her toothbrush; it lay, still damp, on the washbasin. He reached out to touch it, and then drew his hand back quickly. He returned to the bedroom and sat down on the bed and fumbled on the bed table for a match and felt the ring. It was no longer warm. He picked it up without looking at it, and wrapped it in several layers of tissue, and dropped it into the wastebasket. Why did it always have to be raining when one said goodbye, he thought. Why did it always have to be raining?

He removed his shoes and walked into the sitting room. He stood on the brocaded loveseat and took down the picture, gently blowing away the thin wash of dust on the upper molding. With infinite care he pried open the frame, removed the print, and replaced the vacant frame above the loveseat. He returned to the bedroom, and covered the print with smoothed-out tissue, and carefully placed it facedown in his suitcase. He finished his drink, and went into the bathroom and cleaned his teeth. Then he lay down on the loveseat, dangling his legs over the side, and closed his eyes. It was raining again, his plane left early in the morning, and he had a long way to go, a very long way.

Requiem

✤   It is always the same. I am walking down the rusting iron steps of some sort of elevated railway station, which means it must be a dream because I have lived all my life on the Eastern Shore where my father, a failure, lived and died an associate professor of art history at the local college. I do not know what has brought me to this place, or why I am here. All I know is that it is dusk and it is silent except for the scraping of my shoe soles against the rusting iron steps, a sound not unlike the crunching of boots against dry snow, which sets my teeth on edge. The black bumpy handrailing is cold to my touch, although it is late spring, and the air is stained with the smell of rusting iron and soiled under-

garments and dust. As the last clattering sounds of the
train fade I pause and look back at the curving tracks,
hardly visible now in the gathering darkness.

It always ends here. But this time I hesitate in the silence, and listen, halfway down the gritty iron stairway,
scraping my feet in the litter of cigarette stubs, chewing
gum wrappers, smeared tissues and an occasional drying
blister of slime hawked up from sick city lungs. Just as
I turn to retrace my steps to the depot which straddles
the darkened street like a spiderweb of concrete and
iron and rot-dry wood, something happens. I have come
this far, I hear myself saying, I have come this far. I descend the steps quickly, and walk across the street. The
surface is soft and spongy, as though it had been simmering for hours under a midsummer sun. It is almost as though *things* were moving beneath the surface, moving quietly and urgently beneath the dismal
city street.

Cars are parked along the curbing. I step gingerly
between a laundry van and a pizza-mobile, cross the
sidewalk, and hesitate before the smudged window of a
small stationery store. I regard my own blurred image
with little satisfaction. A face more gray than tanned in
the waning light, right eye a shade lower than the left
(a family stigmata of which my father had been as
proud as though it were the harelip of a Hapsburg),
nose broken twice and twice carelessly mended by our
family doctor back home, crooked chin only partly concealed by the rough reddish beard ("Van Gogh," my
father had snorted; "by God, you look like a bad imitation of Van Gogh," and with angry, nervous steps withdrew to his study).

I straighten my black knit tie and smooth down the

wilted lapels of my shapeless seersucker coat. I squint at the litter behind the dirt-streaked window: writing tablets, bookbags, pencil sharpeners, cheap ballpoint pens on faded display cards, a jumble of nondescript paperback books, oblong kits containing plastic parts for airplanes and old fashioned automobiles, and a lifesized plastic model of a human head, sliced in half, the pink and gray brain exposed like some great indecent mushroom—and then, on a small shelf, a brightly painted tin monkey with a grinning, impudent face, a monkey dressed like Johnny in the old Philip Morris ads, in a pillbox cap, glaring red and gold-button jacket, and yellow-striped bright blue trousers, a monkey with clasped hands and feet, with a black string running through them, the kind of monkey that when you fasten one end of the string somewhere, say, to a doorknob or the back of a chair or something similar, and then pull the other end of the string, somehow with marvelous jerking movements the monkey climbs the string, hesitating here and halting there but climbing, always climbing. You used to be able to buy a monkey like this for a dime in the dimestore back home, but it has been years since I have seen one of them.

Then I realize that I am being watched.

An ugly, fat, baldheaded man in shirt sleeves and black apron appears out of nowhere. From the dark well of his dingy shop he peers at me with neither interest nor dislike. Then, saying nothing, indeed making no sign that I even exist, he pulls down a sleazy dark green curtain or shade of some sort. Thin washes of light trickle around the edges of the shade, and then they too disappear as the fat man switches off the lights in the shop.

Damned bastard, I say to myself, damned . . . ; with difficulty I suppress the forbidden monosyllable that leaps to my mind. I walk away from the shop, my cheeks are burning with resentment. I continue to walk, very quickly, so quickly that I soon have to stop to catch my breath. Again I curse the fat, gross man who has so unceremoniously dismissed me. I think of the pleasant merchants and businessmen back home, and their friendly shops on the tree-shaded square.

"What a stinking place this is," I say aloud. "To hell with it."

I start to retrace my steps to the elevated depot, but then, out of nowhere, I hear a familiar sound which breaks the stillness as startlingly as the cracking of the time barrier. Somewhere down the darkening street someone is playing Mozart, a Mozart piano sonata, the Eleventh, I think, as I stand and listen to the familiar sounds, the A major. The notes rise like mist in this veldt of stone and steel, unbelievably pure and clean in the heavy air (rank with the lingering pungence of urine . . . or could it be a similar scent of boxwood, young boxwood?). The music is spritely yet touched with the knowledge of grief, so simple, seemingly, yet so complex: each note is a drop of water falling upon the still surface of a green pond.

I scratch my beard and look over my shoulder in the direction of the depot, and hesitate but a moment. Then I turn my back on the darkness which brought me here. I follow the music until I am standing in front of a row of brownstone houses which look exactly like some of the houses in *Breakfast at Tiffany's*. I scan them with mingled recognition and apprehension:

four, or are they five, stories high, with small out-
cropping ledges or balconies fronting the upper-story
windows and each house with a black iron fence and
gate which apparently leads to a stamp-sized concrete
courtyard, each with its solid, prosperous-looking stone
steps ascending to a second-story entrance. Surprisingly
(are not all cities filled with children?) there are no
children, no signs or sounds of children, no sounds, indeed, of any sort except the rise and fall of my own
asthmatic breathing and the flowing loveliness of the
Mozart.

The house before which I am standing is very much
like the others except for the fact that in front of it, on
the sidewalk near the curb, there stands a black steel
hitching post topped with the arched head of a horse
with a ring in his mouth (there are still one or two of
these on the Square back home, though of course they
are never used). Like ornamental gas lamps, such
hitching posts have recently become very *camp* and can
be bought at shops along the highways together with
gaudily painted Negro stableboys and hideous pink fla-
mingos or paralyzed-looking white-rabbit families of
painted concrete. I am sure that this hitching post was
not purchased at such a place, and walk towards it. I
avoid the sparse dried droppings near the curb; as far as
I am concerned they do not exist. At the same time I
know instinctively, surely, that something is moving
beneath the pavement, a quickness, a restlessness which
can be felt throughout my body. It is as though seeds
were germinating beneath the surface, a stirring which
is both felt and audible to the inner ear and which is
matched by a similar awareness that somewhere far

above the dusty streets water is flowing, flowing, flowing, while a great wheel, moss covered and dripping, is slowly turning in some enormous millpond.

Now I hesitate only a moment at the single step which descends from the sidewalk to the tiny courtyard which fronts the tall, narrow house. Three or four strides and to my right is a black iron grillwork door with a chipped porcelain doorknob which is cold to my touch. Behind the door is an open space of some sort, a dark areaway, but when I squint into the darkness I can, finally, distinguish what appear to be some receptacles of some sort or other, garbage pails perhaps, and then, and my heart leaps with delight, a sled, its runners propped against the wall, a Flexible Flyer, I imagine, from the curving arch of its head.

The sled delights and reassures me. My anger at the gross fat man has subsided, along with the crawling sense of apprehension which has been stirring in my viscera since I left the depot. Where there is a sled there must be children, or a child, and I try once again to open the door, but the chipped doorknob is unyielding. I step back into the tiny yard. Above my head, the music seems to be dying away. As I look up, searching for the source of the whispering, a finger of light beckons me from beyond the curtained second-floor windows. I mount the steps and stand before a massive door with a stout brass doorknob and a magnificent rococo brass knocker in the form of a gargoyle's head.

The doorknob turns very easily. I stand in a small vestibule floored in inlaid tile. A second, inner door is invitingly ajar, so I step quietly into the house. A long green-carpeted hallway extends, apparently, the length of the house and becomes lost in shadows; so too does the carpeted flight of stairs which disappears into upper darkness. To my right is an elaborately carved mahogany chest over which hangs an oblong mirror the size and dimensions of a coffin. Alongside the chest is an empty clothes tree and beside it an umbrella stand. To my left, flush against the green carpet, faintly etched with some sort of fleur-de-lis pattern, is a pair of sliding doors. Beyond the doors the last notes of the sonata fade away into the whispered recollection of a memory.

I push these apart and am immediately dwarfed by the enormous gilt-framed mirror which extends from a few feet above the gleaming floor to the high ceiling. Before the mirror, on a marble ledge, stand several porcelain figure groups, Meissen or Viennese I cannot tell, but they are of such admirable artistry that I would not be surprised were they the work of Grassi or some comparable master. With uplifted sword, St. George threatens a writhing, forked-tongued dragon, a cavalier and his lady sit comfortably astride a pair of magnificent matched bays, and a frock-coated, periwigged lover leans over his mistress whose plump bosoms are revealed rather than concealed by the lacy fan she holds in a shapely white hand so lifelike that when I reach out and gently stroke it I am shocked by its cold, unyielding contours.

Reluctantly I turn from the lovers and step softly from one Bokhara rug to another, small oblong islands of richly subdued color in the sea of the inlaid parquet floor. The walls, cool blue, are hung with gilt-framed paintings of nymphs and satyrs and pink-fleshed goddesses, but I do not linger here. Near an arch at the end of the long drawing room I glimpse high walnut bookcases; I enter the library as though I had known this room all my life. On the walls are a water-color of the Rotunda of the University of Virginia and the familiar steel engraving, once found in almost every respectable Southern home, of Lee and Jackson, mounted, on the field of battle. Unlike the drawing room with its silks and satins, gilded armchairs and diminutive French sofas, the furniture in the library is solid, comfortable, dependable. I sit down on a dark green leather couch, the kind one would find in a fraternity house or in the commons room of a nineteenth-century gentlemen's club. Against the glass-doored bookcase in front of me is a Shakespearean group in bisque, so popular in my grandfather's day but very seldom seen now except in antique or curio shops: Romeo with great grace approaches his Juliet who averts her cheek ever so slightly, more in acquiescence than rejection, while her nurse, sly procuress, regards both lovers with knowing inquisitiveness. Then and only then, hanging over the comfortable leather couch at the far end of the room, do I see another picture, a painting which makes my stomach turn. This monstrosity is either an affront or a bad joke or an unforgivable blunder.

I am looking at a large, meticulously painted copy of what my father once called the most revolting painting in existence, Rembrandt's "The Anatomy Lesson of Dr. Tulp." I avert my eyes from it in disgust, sickened by the cadaver's pale, hard flesh, so hairless, rigid, and obscene in its irrevocable lifelessness. I can smell the death in the pitiful, half-open mouth, and the exposed red flesh and corded tendons of the violated, ravished arm evoke memories of Dachau and Buchenwald. Gagging, I hasten from the library, and almost stumble

into the now-silent record player which led me here in
the first place. Beyond the doorway I pause, why I am
not sure; something in me says, stop, wait. In front of
me is a towering walnut bookcase. Behind its glassed
doors I recognize large octavos, magnificently bound in
ivory-colored linen and stamped in gold, black and
scarlet. Without hesitating, I turn the brass key and
swing open the door, and trace my fingers over the
smooth surface of the Old Manse edition of Haw-
thorne; they stop at Volume 18, the *American Note-
books*. I remove the book carefully and place it on top
of the record player and carefully, carefully, open it. A
faint dry odor tantalizes my nostrils and brings back
memories of my father's study back home. I look for
several moments at the autographed frontispiece,
Harry Fenn's watercolor of cloud-shrouded Gray Lock,
a simple painting, but majestic in its simplicity: sky,
clouds, mountain, a meadow with a flock of sheep (curiously, but not grotesquely, their heads look to the
mountain, their hindquarters address the viewer), a
meandering stream, a triangle of lush grass and spring
flowers. A slip of paper protrudes half-way through the
book; I turn to page 265 and read aloud the familiar
words, faintly outlined in pencil: *Some most secret
thing, valued and honored between lovers, to be hung
up in public places, and made the subject of remark by
the city,—remarks, sneers, and laughter.* Curious, I
think, and turn the page: a faded photograph falls to
the floor like an autumn leaf, twisting and turning so I
catch only a quick glimpse of a young woman's profile,
her hair done up in an elaborate bun beneath a mon-
strous Gibson Girl hat.

As I stoop to retrieve it, I hear behind me a light

step and I am suddenly aware of subdued breathing and the faint scent of lemon lilies. I turn guiltily, a child surprised at the cookie jar. A young woman stands before me. Her hair is aglow in the winking light of a candelabrum which she holds aloft, above and to the right of her fair forehead. Her parted lips are as inviting as early spring strawberries, but there is the beginning of a frown between her arched eyebrows. Except for this she seems so typically the personal maid of English country house comedy that I would not be at all surprised were she to say, "La, sir," and make a perfunctory curtsy, but as she steps closer to me I see that her lashes are beaded with mascara, and artfully applied violet shadows accentuate eyes whose irises are the color of the flesh of a honeydew melon.

For a long moment she looks at me without speaking. Her pale green eyes are flecked with gold; the pupils are slightly dilated. Slowly she lowers her upraised arm, the flames of the candles flicker away from me, beneath her fresh gray uniform—incongruously, the name "Cherry" is spelled out in dark blue running script over her breast—she owns a beautiful body. I stroke my beard again, and start to speak, but she raises her hand as if in warning. Her frown has disappeared and her eyes seem warm with recognition.

"Why did you come?" she says in a voice like Shakespeare's Cordelia. "Why are you here?"

The directness of the question startles me. "Please," I say, irritated at the uncertainty in my voice. I make a slightly helpless, upward movement of my hands. "Please," I say again, "I heard the Mozart, and followed it here, and, well, the door was open." I smile at her. "That's about it, I guess. The door was ajar, so I came in. That's about it."

"Oh," she says, and places the candelabrum on a table. I start to speak, but she places a tapered finger against her lips and raises her eyebrows ever so slightly. Incredibly, then, she comes to me, she is in my arms, and the lights are dimming all along the long walls of the rococo room. Voiceless, she follows me to one of the soft, small couches, but it will not bear our weight, so we go to the large dark-green couch in the library. Everything of her is beautiful and wonderful and desirable, strange and at the same time familiar; the sudden open mouth of assent and the swift, sweet tongue of love; beneath the chaste uniform everything is warm and alive and good, the knowing nipple and the willing, open secret place.

As I enter her she closes her eyes and smiles in the dark; so sweet, she whispers, so sweet, but then the silence is shattered by a sudden pealing and jangling. Beneath us, in the dark lower reaches of the vast house, below and behind us bells are ringing, ringing in the darkness as though they will never stop.

Cherry's body twists beneath me. I try to prevent her escape, my knee pressed between her still open thighs, one of my hands slipping from her golden, lovely head. It is too late. She is free from me, free of me. Separate and alone she smiles down upon me, and touches one finger to her bruised lips and traces my forehead with it, ever so gently. Then she turns her back to me. She makes silent smoothing movements with her hands, rearranging her tossed hair, restoring rustling order to her skirt and petticoats. I lie there dead. I look for the last time at the open-mouthed, barrel-chested cadaver above me. The bells continue to ring, and Cherry touches my cold hand with her warm fingers. I get up and follow her to the hallway. At the head of the dark stairs she turns and again places a warning finger against her lips. She nods in the direction of the sounds. We are in total darkness now, but I can see her lips frame the words *come with me.*

I am tired, incomplete, diminished, but I follow her dumbly into the pit. At the foot of the stairs I have an impulse to pull open the door, rush through the dark areaway—will the sled still be there, unused, unwanted, forgotten?—and escape into the street, but Cherry's hand, surprisingly strong, closes around my wrist.

Come, she is saying (again in the darkness her lips frame the words which I can see but not hear); you must come with me.

There is no escape now, I realize, so I follow her down the long, bare hall. She stops before a door beyond which the bells are ringing, a cascade of sound, an orgasm of sleighbells echoing and reechoing up and down the draughty corridor.

Cherry pushes the door open and stands aside in a curtsy only half mocking, her right hand describing a gracefully descending arc. I hesitate but she nudges my elbow and I step reluctantly into the kitchen. My heart is tumbling. Have I been expecting a Charles Addams interior with vaulted cobwebby ceiling and vast fireplace with steaming witches' cauldron, and God knows what unnamed horrors festering in dark corners? But this is a prosaic room: blue and white linoleum-covered floor, white porcelain refrigerator, electric dishwasher and stove upon which a saucepan is simmering. The room is empty, except for the ringer of the bells, an old, old lady with short-cropped hair more iron gray than white. In one hand she grasps a rawhide thong which runs through three champagne-colored sleighbells the size and shape of English walnuts, sleighbells which she is impatiently shaking so that the entire kitchen is flowing with sound. In the other hand she holds a gold chain to which is attached an oval gold locket.

The old lady is confined to an aluminum wheelchair, securely and painlessly imprisoned by a stout strap or belt of some sort and further confined by a tray very much like that on a child's old fashioned high-chair. As I stand before her, open mouthed, she drops the sleigh-bells to the floor and carefully lays the locket on the tray. She ignores me completely, or does not see me, but makes fluttering movements with her hands at Cherry who has noiselessly stepped between me and the old lady. She chirps like a sparrow and points to the saucepan on the clean stove.

"Yes, lover," Cherry says. "I know you're hungry. Be a good girl and we'll have your supper in three shakes of a lamb's tail."

She goes to the stove, stopping on the way to bend over and quickly kiss the iron-gray head. She removes the lid from the pan and stirs the contents with a wooden spoon as steam drifts slowly towards the ceiling and the spicy scent makes my mouth water. Very quietly I pull a chair close to the old lady and sit down beside her. She turns her old face in my direction, but the faded, mad gray eyes do not see me. It is a good face, the kind of face my mother's might have become, had she lived. High cheekbones and what my grand-father would have called a handsome Macbeth nose, a patrician face except for the slack and bloodless lips, a face that has seen everything and forgotten everything. She stares through me for a long time. The room is quiet except for the gentle simmering sound from the saucepan.

I start to say something, but I am suddenly aware of Cherry's disapproval. I look at her as she turns swiftly from the stove and raises an ominous finger. She shakes her head and her full lips frame a single unspoken *no*. I nod in acquiescence, and she goes back to the stove. I turn again to the old lady whose hands suddenly descend like doves to her tray; there, her fingers flutter as though in pain, until they stop on the smooth, rounded surface of the locket. She caresses the tarnished gold surface with hands which once must have been as shapely as snowflakes, hands so beautiful that a lover would involuntarily turn them over and place them palm up within his own and stroke ever so gently with warm fingertips, hands like a woman in miniature, of the shape and texture of love with their soft hills and valleys and tapering thigh-like fingers, hands so beautiful that the heart weeps that time could reduce them to these sad claws of bone and parchment. Gently, so gently, the bent fingers stroke the locket, trembling over the engraved tracing of entwined roses, pausing to explore the familiar dented surface.

We are forgotten completely, Cherry who is now spooning the spicy porridge into a china bowl, and I, sitting beside her, looking at the poor imprisoned body, so frail that beneath the tidy housedress with its faint dry odor of starch and laundry soap you can discern its birdlike skeleton, the shrunken rib cage, the useless legs, and the tired little feet half lost within the gray felt nests of their bedroom slippers. She is so still that I think she has fallen asleep or died, poor soul, there in her own small prison, but now she turns her head towards me and her sightless eyes wander over my face and then, suddenly, stop. Is she beckoning to me, calling or trying to communicate with me, suddenly wise and knowing?

"What is it, dear heart?" I hear myself whispering. "What is it, poor little mother?"

She does not answer, but again her hands flutter to the locket. Her pale lips are moving, trembling. She, too, is whispering, urgently, desperately. I bend towards her, incline my ear to her lips and at the same time reach for the locket, but one dry hand closes over my own while she continues to stroke its surface with the other. She continues to whisper; I can feel the faint expiration of her breath in my ear, but I cannot distinguish any sounds.

"What is it, dear heart?" I say again, and lean forward, exploring for the locket which I must see, but I hear Cherry's light, firm steps, and I draw back. Cherry carries a bowl of the spicy porridge, a Spode cup and saucer, for tea, and a small silver pitcher of milk or cream. She stands between me and the locket; as far as she is concerned I no longer exist. With swift, deft movement she transfers the bowl, the cup and saucer, and the pitcher to the tray, pushing the locket to one side. The old lady is chirping with excitement; she tilts back her head, raising her chin aloft, and opens her lips like a bird, eagerly awaiting the porridge. Cherry feeds her expertly, spooning the porridge into the eager mouth and gently wiping the slack lips with a tiny napkin. I reach out and touch Cherry's upper arm; she shrugs my hand aside and continues her chore.

"Cherry," I whisper. "Who is she, the little mother?"

The old lady quickly turns her head in my direction.

She raises her arm at the same time and the porridge-filled spoon spins out of Cherry's hand and clatters against the floor.

"Now you've done it," Cherry cries, and I am shocked by the venom in her voice. "Now you've done it for fair, you fool, you!"

She seizes the napkin and stoops over to mop up the mess. The old lady raps her tray with one impatient hand while she strokes the locket with the other. Then, with infinite care, she raises the locket to eye level. She studies it intently before lowering it to her lips. She kisses it silently and drops it to her tray as Cherry approaches her chair. She again starts to feed the old lady and looks at me over her shoulder.

You fool, her lips say. We do not want you here. Why did you come?

"I came to find the child," I say. I whistle with astonishment at the words the moment they are uttered.

Cherry strikes the tray with open palm. The milk pitcher and bowl tremble.

"The child?" she cries. "What child?"

She looks at me coldly; how, just a few minutes ago—or was it hours—could I have thought those eyes were warm and full of love? The pupils are frightfully shrunken, they seem no larger than the head of a pin, and the pale green irises are remote and frigid.

"There is no child here," she says, each word intent yet incredibly distant. We are, all three of us, isolated by barriers of hatred and indifference and age, Cherry, cold and trembling with anger; the old lady mewing for her supper, her spirit frozen within her frail flesh; and I, broken-nosed, goat-bearded, and one-eyed, imprisoned in a maze of endless corridors, a cave with no exit.

"No child here!" I cry. "You lie, Cherry!"

Without thinking, unhesitating, surely and swiftly, I cross the room and open the cabinet directly above the sink. It is getting dark in the kitchen, almost imperceptibly the lights are dimming, but my hands are certain. I ignore the smooth impersonal surface of a china cup, touch and quickly abandon the cylindrical nothingness of glasses, welcome for an instant and then reject the rococo umbilicus of a silver sugar bowl. Then, triumphantly, my fingers arrive at their destination. My fingers explore the familiar mystery, the round pillbox hat, the grinning face, the jointed arms and legs, the stout torso and the coiled rubber tail, the slack string between clasped hands and feet. I withdraw the monkey and confront Cherry. I thrust it before her eyes, a priest with crucifix holding at bay the medieval demon. She steps back and I take a long breath to calm the thumping of my heart.

"You lie, Cherry," I say again.

She does not answer, but continues to stare at me with her cold eyes. For a moment I think she is going to spit upon me. Then her shoulders droop; the anger passes from her eyes and mouth.

"No child," she says. She no longer cares, all vitality is drained from her.

I point to the monkey.

"How can you have a monkey and no child? And the sled? What of the sled?"

I wave the monkey in front of her eyes, but her hand intercepts my own. Her fingers tighten around my wrist. God, she is strong; the monkey falls from my hand and clatters to the floor. She continues to squeeze my wrist, and the frill of lace at the cuff of her starched gray uniform leaves her own wrist exposed. It is a strong, masculine wrist; swart, coarse hairs sprout lewdly against her frog-speckled skin. I make a quick backward lunge; my hand is free. I retrieve the monkey, and put it into the pocket of my seersucker jacket. Panting, I look at her with contempt.

"No children," she says, and walks slowly from the room. I am left alone with the old lady who places one hand over the locket, one dry arm resting on the tray, the other dangling at her side. She looks at me for a moment before laying her head on her arm. In a moment she is asleep; I edge to her and touch her shoulder tentatively, gently; the frail bones are as empty as those of a dead bird. Slowly I lower my hand and place it over hers; ever so gently, I think, I will disengage her hand and free the locket from its prison. She shudders slightly when my hand brushes against hers, and I quickly withdraw. When her breathing becomes regular again I hover over her, and a ludicrous and frightening image leaps into my mind's eye: the crisis scene from *The Phantom of the Opera* my hands the beloved one the young singer hers the phantom stealthily dishonorably I intend to violate my promise his fingers are caressing the keyboard of the organ deep in the funereal and forbidden chambers in the ultimate bowels of l'Opéra his back is to me black somber but he is alive with love I tiptoe towards the goal I must penetrate the mystery I must remove the mask my fingers tremble because now they are only inches away he shifts on the bench and raises his fingers from the keys the magic he has created dies away he reaches out and briefly caresses my hand and turns once more to the keyboard with pretense of innocence I retreat again he is lost in his love dreams the chamber swells with his released passion and again I steal behind him burning to betray to look now finally the supreme moment the moment of truth I tear off the mask and the vaulted room is alive with shrieks and howls he leaps from his bench growing towering towards the vaulted ceiling his betrayed face compounded of nightmare and anguish the few thin strands of lank hair plastered against the skull-like forehead the shapeless nose obscene pits in a desert of desolation.

I reach for the old lady, lift up the dry hand, and remove the locket unprotested; she continues to doze in her prison. As I fumble with the clasp, I hear Cherry reenter the room and quickly I put the locket in my pocket.

"Oh, go ahead if you must," Cherry says.

I remove it from my pocket, and again try to open it. Cherry takes it from my hand and opens it easily, as one would open a prayer book or a hymnal.

"You are a fool," she says and hands it to me. I peer through the scratched glass, gray with age and as criss-crossed with faint scratches as the wrinkled cheek resting on the frail arm beside me. A cry of disappointment escapes my lips. Hastily I close the locket and place it back on the tray. I look at Cherry, who is standing apart and aloof, divorced from the action. The old lady does not stir.

"Little mother, little mother," I say when I can find my voice. "Forgive me, dear heart."

I put my hand lightly on her thin shoulder and with my free hand I quietly stroke her hand which once again has closed over the locket. We sit there together, completely quiet, for a long time. Now it is completely dark, and there are no sounds anywhere, except finally

I think I hear a door close somewhere above my head. Only then do I gently disengage myself. I take a final farewell of the bowed dark stillness in the chair. For the last time, I brush the dry hair with my lips, and tiptoe out of the kitchen. I walk slowly down the bare, dark hall till I come to the staircase. I hesitate for a moment, undecided whether to leave as I had entered or through the vestibule with the quiet sled. I shrug my shoulders and try to swallow, but my throat is painfully dry. I turn away from the dark cave, and ascend the stairs. I walk slowly down the long, richly-carpeted corridor, and pause for a moment before the dark shape, palpable against the greater darkness, of the hatrack. Cherry, invisible, is waiting for me; once again the air is warm with the remembrance of the odor of lemon lilies, stirring slightly with the ghost of the Mozart piano sonata. Before she can open the inner door I slip my arm around her hard waist and pull her to me. I try to open her cold lips but they are thousands of miles away.

Roughly I open the inner door, quickly cross through the vestibule, my feet slipping slightly on its tiled surface, twist open the cold brass knob of the outer door, and descend the steps. Only for an instant do I turn and look back at the dark and empty house, before feeling my way cautiously to the curb. There are no lights anywhere, no sounds. I pick my way slowly along the unyielding sidewalk till my feet touch grass and, finally, gravel. Of course, I can see nothing, absolutely nothing, but I know that there are great ditches on either side of me. In the ditches there are dreadful forms and shapes, of many children, some of them sleeping with wide, unseeing eyes, some of them eyeless, others tongueless, children diseased and gross and beautiful, children with twisted bodies and starved unhappy hearts. In the darkness, alone in this black place, I gradually become aware of sounds, faint, faraway sounds, a long, slowly diminishing wailing. I struggle to find the mouth of the cave, but the darkness thickens around me, settling heavily to the ground until the moaning of the children is inaudible and I cannot even hear the grating sound of the gravel beneath my feet.

The Pilgrims

Theo awakened painfully, Penrod's tongue rough on his bare arm. His head ached from too many drinks and the sleeping pill Lee-Anna had given him a few hours before, and his nose and throat were dry. During the night he had slipped from his accustomed propped-up sleeping position, and the intricate maze of his sinuses seemed permanently blocked. He fumbled among the rumpled bedding for his decongestant nasal mist inhalant; after a moment of irritation he retrieved the oblong container and gratefully inserted the tip into one nostril, and squeezed. A slow loosening, he knew, would soon take place. Grudgingly, reluctantly, the interior fretwork of canals and viaducts would expand, and he could breathe again.

Now Penrod was licking his face with fiercely affectionate sloshings, and Theo groaned and turned over on the sofa-bed and tried to hide his face. But the lemon-hued burlap—very big that spring, Lee-Anna had cried triumphantly while she was making the slipcover, very camp—scratched his cheeks, so he turned again and placed one shaky hand on Penrod's woolly, misshapen head. I feared that we might regret this act of kindness, he thought, recalling slowly the blurred events of the past evening. Such a dog! Lee-Anna's poet-husband Horatio, an admirer of Somerset Maugham, had suggested that they name him Philip Carey, after they discovered that one of the dog's hind paws was deformed, but he and Lee-Anna had immediately scotched *that* idea. And the banty? What had they finally decided to name it? Octavio Paz? James Baldwin? Roderick Random? No, that had been Horatio's idea, too. He and Lee-Anna had voted *that* down. And then compromised. Usher, that was it. Roderick Usher.

"Lee-Anna," he called softly. "Lee-Anna, Horatio."

He lay very still and waited. The inhalant was beginning to take effect. Sunlight was slowly penetrating the dark caves in his skull. He explored slowly the rough contours of Penrod's head, gently inserted a finger into one hairy ear, traced the masses of corkscrew curls which fringed the bony eyesockets, and finally placed his hand in the friendly mouth.

He's ugly, Theo thought, but really rather sweet. So gentle and so happy last night when we rescued him from the Kiwanians. With difficulty he opened one eye but closed it quickly at the sight of the hobgoblin head a few inches from his own. What a monster, he thought, a ragtag and bobtail if there ever was one, a curly-haired, taffy-colored fleabag of beggar's-lice, cockleburrs, and milkweed seeds.

"What asses the Kiwanians were last night," he cried aloud. "Lee-Anna, the Kiwanians are asses!"

Delighted at the sound of life going on around him, Penrod sprang clumsily to the bed, and again Theo tried to bury his face in the covers. He's sweet but oh so *gauche,* he thought, and *country,* too; if a dog could have hayseed in his ears, Penrod would. Who but the Kiwanians would have the temerity to palm off such a dog as a door prize? Penrod and that scrawny little bantam rooster?

At the recollection he sat upright.

"Lee-Anna, Horatio," he called. "Are you awake? Where is the banty? Where, in the name of Heaven, is the young cock, Roderick?"

For several moments he lay motionless, listening for the familiar voices. Apart from the quiet ebb and flow of what seemed to be ditchwater between his ears, and the huff-chuff-huff of Penrod's breathing, the small house was quiet, uncomfortably so. Could they be dead, he mused, Lee-Anna and Horatio? Of ptomaine poisoning, perhaps? Quite possible. He played with the idea the way he sometimes entertained his Life and Literature students with explications of the Baconian theory, comments on Baudelaire's use of drugs, or analyses of the friendship between Beaumont and Fletcher. The salami, he recalled painfully, his stomach turning, had looked green at the time, and who but the Kiwanians would serve ham hocks at a buffet? We should never have gone to their party, he thought.

"It never pays for town and gown to fraternize," he announced loudly.

Penrod again placed his great paws on the edge of the sofa-bed and noisily began to lick Theo's forehead. The rough tongue has become a dentist's drill, Theo thought. Soon he will be tearing the skin, in a few minutes the scalp will be exposed; it will unpeel, like the layers of an onion, revealing all the terrible inner workings, all the pulsing pink—or are they gray?—lobes, and all the hideous hills and valleys.

"Lee-Anna," he called again, more feebly. Could she and Horatio have been murdered in their sleep? Ever since Capote's account of the Clutter murders one could never be sure of *anything*. And in a faculty housing compound particularly. Some surly physicist could easily run amok, enraged at Horatio's penchant for midnight guitar-playing or Lee-Anna's fondness for tight stretchpants, staggeringly high heels, and exposed midriff. Or a marauding freshman from Remedial English, maddened at having recently received a midterm deficiency. More than possible, Theo reflected. Indeed, quite as likely as not. But not a bad way to go, actually, when you come right down to it. Or perhaps Lee-Anna had simply died in her sleep. It would serve her right, in a way. After all, it was she who had insisted that they go to the buffet. Just because her employer was a Kiwanian . . . . She didn't *have* to accept the invitation to the bloody buffet. Or, having accepted, to insist that Horatio and he accompany her. And what a stupid, tacky thing to do. At midnight, to raffle off a dog. And a bantam rooster!

Again he opened his eyes and squinted painfully at the massive, curl-encrusted head. None of the Kiwanians, of course, would accept the dog, or the rooster either, for that matter. The banty? Where was it? He had a confused recollection that Roderick had been perched upon his head when they finally left the hotel. A dour and bedraggled devil, but Lee-Anna had insisted. And how the bird stank! Like all the chicken-houses of Boone, Howard, and Calloway counties combined. Probably would give all of them histoplasmosis. He had been cute, though, perched aloft that way.

A sentimentalist at heart, Lee-Anna had insisted that they take the unwanted pair home with them. We simply must, she had exclaimed when none of the Kiwanians would accept them as door prizes. We simply must, she had repeated in a whiskey-high voice, we simply must! And so they had finally staggered out of the Daniel Boone Hotel, Lee-Anna and Horatio supporting the half-fainting Penrod and he, Theo, with Roderick Usher precariously clinging to his head.

I can still feel those toenails, Theo thought. And that *smell!* It was cute, though, the way he took to me. But where, in the name of Heaven, *is* he?

He explored the end of the bed with his toes, and searched beneath the flimsy blanket with which Lee-Anna had tucked him in—you must not go back to your apartment tonight, Theo, she had said, must he, lamb-a-baum?—and finally pushed Penrod away and leaned over the bed to examine the floor. The effort was costly. His head felt like an overripe melon and he was gagging in the sudden rise of bile to his throat.

"Lee-Anna!" he called again. "Horatio! Water, for the love of God, water!"

In the silence he waited with growing impatience.

"They flee from me that sometime did me seek."

He spoke the words testily. They must be dead or ill, he thought, and reached over and ran his hand over Penrod's tousled head. Ah, well, I have the dog. He will not desert me. And Roderick Usher, too, I trust. They, my friends of the air and the land, will stay by me, even though my human companions have defected. I was fond of Horatio and Lee-Anna, too. But I can do without them. I would have gone through fire and water for Lee-Anna, though.

"Preferably water, however," he announced aloud, and straightened out his bony legs. I shall die here myself in all likelihood, he reflected. Here in Hell's Half Acre, in this miserable crackerbox of a house for instructors-without-tenure. Exhausted at the idea, he closed his eyes and crossed his hands upon his chest, and listened to Penrod's labored pantings beneath the bed. Images of Landseer paintings of great faithful dogs keeping midnight vigil at their masters' graves flitted through his mind, and a crooked smile briefly illuminated his somber features. What a truly great dog Penrod is, he thought. So full of affection, so grateful to have found a home at last. He reached again for the mass of curls beneath the bed. If I too must die, what better way to go? No more freshman themes to grade, no more seminars to struggle through, no language requirements, no doctoral dissertation to write. I shall die here with my friends, Lee-Anna and Ray. Here with commitment. Commitment and love. I shall close my eyes and await the end . . . .

A groan from the bedroom on the other side of the thin wall interrupted his reveries. He struggled painfully to a sitting position while Penrod, alarmed, squirmed from beneath the sofa-bed.

"Lee-Anna," he whispered. "Ray. Is it really you?"

A second groan followed by a paroxysm of coughing confirmed his hopes.

"Oh, praise God, they are both alive. You have survived. Bless you, bless you both!"

He gazed fondly at Penrod. The dog had turned over on his back, hind legs sprawled apart, front paws wildly waving as though stirring an imaginary bowl of egg whites.

"Up, boy, up!" Theo grasped one shaggy paw and squeezed it. "Up, I say! All's well with the world, sir. All's well with the world!"

II

"What a curse," Theo lamented two hours and three Bloody Marys later. "To have a chicken fall in love with you. Really! Don't misunderstand me," he added to Lee-Anna who lay on the rumpled bed, her blonde, short-cropped head in his lap. "I appreciate Roderick's judgment and discrimination."

He gestured with his thumb at the bantam who was perched on his shoulder, its moulting body against Theo's neck, its ravaged head close to his cheek. Gingerly Theo touched the rooster's spongy, drooping comb with his forefinger, and the cock immediately rose on saffron-colored toes, flapped one scrawny wing, threw back its head and uttered a strange and terrible cry.

"You see?" Theo sighed and reached for the Bloody Mary which was precariously balanced on Lee-Anna's naked midriff. "That banshee cry. It's getting me down, baby. If only he'd be quiet for a few minutes. Like Penrod." He pointed to the deformed hind foot protruding from beneath the sofa-bed.

"I'm not sure that I can stand it much longer. And that hot barnyard smell!" Theo shuddered and took a long swallow of the highly-seasoned tomato juice and vodka. "To say nothing of that piercing ancient mariner type eye. It's really beginning to bug me."

He reached down and patted Lee-Anna's head, running his fingers lightly through her soft, dry curls. She was proud of her hair, and spent a lot of time on it, coming up each season with a different colored rinse, and on expensive wigs which Horatio could not afford; they change my personality, she would say, just as Gumbril, Jr. changed his personality when he donned his beaver. She was a great admirer of the early Huxley novels; there has been no comic spirit in English fiction since Huxley finished *Point Counterpoint,* she would insist after she had had a few drinks and the conversation had become literary.

"How is old Ray making out?" Theo glanced in the direction of the bathroom.

"He's still violently ill, I'm afraid. He's been vomiting every few minutes." Lee-Anna arched her carefully plucked eyebrows and looked at Roderick, who had fallen asleep on Theo's shoulder. "Ever since he had to clean out the back seat of the car. Really, Theo, you shouldn't have left him there all night. It really was awful. Smelly feathers everywhere. And all the, uh," she grimaced and patted her lips with her long, tapering fingers, "you know. I never realized chickens could make such a mess. It was really awful. Ray was as white as a sheet when he came in."

"Mess!" Theo cried, putting down his empty glass with such vehemence that Penrod retreated farther beneath the sofa-bed. "Who knows about that better than I? You have to expect that, with chickens. The folks had chickens, back in West Plains. I hated chickens. Besides, honey babe," his voice became less heated, "as I recall, it was your idea to bring him home with us."

Gently he untied the bow at the nape of Lee-Anna's neck and slipped the mauve and cinnamon halter from her plump shoulders.

"You'd be surprised how much a chicken eats and evacuates," he explained. "Back home we had a colored man to take care of them," he continued, and slowly brushed her round little breasts with his fingertips. "But even with that I could do without them. Greedy things," he chuckled and glanced at the dozing bantam, at the same time making a clucking noise with his tongue against the roof of his mouth. The rooster awakened and gazed fondly at Theo before rising on prehensile yellow toes and throwing back his head; again the room reverberated with the hideous cry.

"It's not really the mess, though," he continued, idly watching his fingers in their dainty exploration of Lee-Anna's slightly rounded belly. "Or even the smell, for that matter. It's just that he's so . . . so damned affectionate. If he just wouldn't want to stay so close to me."

He placed one hand, fingers outstretched, around Roderick's arched breast, but the bird shuddered and clamped his toes tightly on the bony ridge of Theo's shoulder.

"You see? Don't ever let a chicken fall in love with you." He stroked Lee-Anna's closed eyelids with his fingertips. "I'm afraid, dear heart, that Roderick is expendable."

"So nice," she whispered, and stirred slightly. "So nice."

"But it's the eyes more than anything else that really get to me."

He withdrew his hand and pointed at Roderick, who had again laid his reptilian head against Theo's cheek and seemed to be peering intently into his left eye. With a sudden impatient upward thrust of his hand Theo swept the bantam from its perch and placed him, squawking and wildly fluttering his good wing, on the inverted v-shaped hollow at the base of Lee-Anna's throat. Penrod, alarmed at Lee-Anna's sudden squeal and the quick upward thrust of her body, scrambled from beneath the sofa-bed and barked hysterically as Lee-Anna tossed Roderick high in the air. The cock descended slowly, with loud cries and frantic flappings, to land, like a sky diver miraculously falling into a mountain of foam rubber, on the massed curls of Penrod's back. In one swift action the dog swung his head, jaws snapping, missing the screaming rooster by a fraction of an inch.

Lee-Anna leaped from the sofa-bed. "Bad dog!" she cried. Roderick had fluttered to the floor where he lay in a heap of feathers, one leg extended grotesquely, the yellow toes rigid.

"Brutal creature!" Theo added, and aimed an angry barefooted kick at Penrod. Tail between his legs and massive head lowered, the dog limped hastily from the room and with a sorrowful groan collapsed on the kitchen floor.

"What in God's name is going on in there?" Horatio's voice, from the bedroom, was feeble and querulous, sounding as though it had been filtered through miles of contaminated water.

"Nothing, lamb-a-baum," Lee-Anna replied quickly.

"It's just Roderick and Penrod. That's all." She leaned over and cupped the rooster in both hands; it gazed at her silently, and stretched out one leg, then the other, before experimentally flapping his good wing. Lee-Anna placed Roderick on the floor gently and clapped her hands in delight as the cock rose unsteadily to his feet, lifted his head, and crowed feebly.

"Good boy, Roderick!" Theo's voice was jubilant as he raised the bantam to his shoulder, shuddering only slightly as the fowl again laid his head against his cheek.

"That was a mean thing to do, Theo," Lee-Anna said, rubbing her throat. "Why did you do that, Theo?"

She was interrupted by the sound of Horatio's footsteps, quickening as he approached the bathroom. The door slammed; they both pretended to ignore the gagging sounds behind it. Finally, in the ensuing quiet, the door opened slowly and Horatio, eyes half closed, felt his way warily into the living room. He squinted at them nearsightedly, swaying slightly, tall and naked except for a too-large pair of seersucker shorts which had slipped down to expose the painfully bony angularities of his hips. Except for his flushed and mottled face, curiously aged for a man in his middle twenties and beaded with drops of perspiration, his skin was as white as milk.

He looked at Lee-Anna and Theo without speaking, moving his lips silently.

"How are you, poor baby?" Lee-Anna, who had deftly rearranged her halter as the sounds of flushing gurgled away in the bathroom, slipped her arm through the crook of Horatio's arm and firmly steered him to the sofa.

"Lie down, lamb-a-baum," she said, and stroked his caved-in appearing temples with deft fingertips.

Again Horatio's lips moved.

"I came like water, and like wind I go," he said weakly, and closed his eyes.

"Why don't you go mix us all some more Bloody Marys, Theo? And be sure to put lots of Worcestershire in them. You know lamb-a-baum likes plenty of Worcestershire."

"It will be my pleasure," Theo said as he walked into the tiny kitchen. Penrod, who had retreated beneath the table, lifted his head and groaned uneasily before limping wearily from the room.

"He flees from me," Theo thought as he poured vodka and tomato juice into a large pitcher. "I who loved him, I who have done him no harm." He mixed the drinks expertly, shaking in the Worcestershire only after he had blended salt, pepper, and lemon juice with the vodka and tomato juice, and returned to the living room. Horatio still lay motionless on the sofa-bed, one pale blue-veined hand resting on Penrod's eyeless-appearing head, while Lee-Anna continued to massage his temples. Theo placed the tray on the coffee table, poured the scarlet drinks into ice-filled glasses, and sat down on the sofa beside Lee-Anna. Penrod stirred uneasily and turned his face from Theo; he snuggled closer to the sofa and placed one great paw on his new master's frail shoulder.

"Well, let's drink to joy," Theo said after a pause.

"To joy," Lee-Anna replied, and touched the rim of her glass against his.

They waited for a response from Horatio, but the poet remained motionless except for his slow exploration of Penrod's head.

"To joy," Theo repeated, more loudly.

Horatio made no answer, but his fingers tightened on his glass. Theo frowned at the recumbent figure on the sofa.

"To joy, dammit," he repeated, and took a swallow of his Bloody Mary before setting the glass on the table so abruptly that the blood-like liquid spilled over the rim and trickled slowly down the sides. "What's bugging you, Ray?" he asked after the silence had become uncomfortable.

"Please, lamb-a-baum." Lee-Anna's voice was as gentle as spring rain. "Don't be sullen, Horatio, please. You know how it upsets me when you're sullen."

The poet continued to gaze at the ceiling before removing Lee-Anna's hand from his forehead. Slowly he raised his glass to his pale lips. He opened his mouth with difficulty, and then drank greedily, his large Adams apple bobbing like a kite on a windy day. When he had drained the glass he again closed his eyes and sighed heavily. Without opening his eyes or turning his head, he extended the empty glass in Theo's direction.

"More," he said, and again sighed a long, asthmatic sigh.

After glancing at Lee-Anna, Theo refilled Horatio's glass and extended it towards the large bony hand which enveloped it in a lover's embrace. Again Horatio drank thirstily and competently before returning the emptied glass to the coffee table. Except for Penrod's labored breathing and the occasional rustling of Roderick's feathers as he twitched uneasily on Theo's shoulder, the room was quiet. In the silence, Theo reached out and patted Lee-Anna's shoulder.

"More," Horatio muttered, extending his hand toward the coffee table. His glass partially refilled, he struggled to a half-sitting position and gazed at Lee-Anna.

"My guitar," he commanded.

"Oh, come off it, Ray," Theo said; "don't order Lee-Anna around that way."

"You hush," Lee-Anna said, and smiled at Horatio who continued to stare at the wall a few inches above her head. "Of course, dear heart."

She rose gracefully, automatically pulling up the straps of her halter, and took the instrument from the litter of books, dog-eared magazines, a collapsed bag-pipe, and a pair of rusting ice skates in one corner of the room. She placed the instrument in her husband's outstretched arms. Head cocked quizzically to one side like a robin listening for worms, he struck a few preliminary chords.

"Ugh," he said, and frowned. His right hand fingers fluttered up and down the offending strings; very carefully he turned the keys.

"I have composed a song," he said, finally satisfied. Exhausted, he carefully placed the instrument at the side of the sofa and fell back upon the rumpled bedding.

"Do sing it, dear heart." Lee-Anna clapped her hands and drained her glass.

"Very good," Theo cried. "Capital! Capital!"

Horatio stared at him coldly for several moments before struggling to a sitting position. Breathing heavily he retrieved the guitar, and gazed into space.

"It's called 'Bulge at the Belly, Nelly'," he announced. He lifted his head, plucked the strings, and began to sing in a good but very shaky tenor.

When I was a little girl
My mother said to me
Come and sit beside me, Nell,
And hearken to my plea.
Beware of men who flatter you
And stroke you so fondly,
Or . . .

The poet's voice quavered and broke, and he glanced imperiously towards the pitcher of Bloody Marys. Lee-Anna poured a short drink into her own emptied glass and held it to Horatio's lips. After a long sip and a mirthless smile, he resumed.

Or
You'll bulge at the belly, Nelly,
Bulge conspicuously.

He closed his eyes and caressed the guitar.

Yes, you'll bulge at the belly, Nelly,
Bulge irrevocably.

He placed the guitar carefully on the floor and lapsed into silence.

"That's very good, Ray! Very fine indeed!" Theo walked to Horatio and patted his shoulder. "Really first-rate, old boy."

Horatio raised himself on one shaky elbow. He stared at Theo blankly.

"Go to hell," he said in a flat, metallic voice, and closed his eyes and fell back. Roderick, suddenly awakened, uttered a hoarse cry, and the alarmed Penrod retreated once again beneath the bed, only his stub tail and deformed paw visible.

"Horatio!" Lee-Anna leaped to her feet, upsetting

her depleted Bloody Mary. "What an ugly way to talk!"

"You're damned right," added Theo. "I don't know what's eating you. Don't start *that* stuff again, Ray!"

Horatio ignored him and squinted at Lee-Anna.

"You have too much makeup on," he said. He put his hands over his eyes and addressed the ceiling. "Why do you insist on going around looking like a small-town B-girl?" He sighed heavily and turned his back to them.

"Knock it off, Ray," Theo said. He turned to Lee-Anna and patted her shoulder. "That's a stupid way to talk, Ray, I must say."

"Yes," Lee-Anna added from the depths of the maize sling chair to which she had retired. "Don't be defensive, darling. You know how you upset me when you're defensive."

"Okay, okay," Horatio said, continuing to address the ceiling. His voice was low, devoid of tone. "Just don't bug me, that's all."

"Knock it off, Ray," Theo said again. He raised a clenched fist in the air, but his voice was gentle. "Tell us a story, or sing or something. Let's not be ugly."

"Well," Ray began, after another long pause. He reached out one hand, fingers outstretched as though searching for the right words. "I recently had a dream."

Theo's clenched fist slowly opened. He lowered his arm, walked to the sofa slowly, and sat down beside the poet. He turned towards Lee-Anna and beckoned. She rose unsteadily, wiping the corners of her eyes, and sat down beside Theo, who put one arm around her shoulders and patted her gently.

"Poor baby. Tell us." She reached out and placed her hand in Horatio's.

"Well," he continued, with a visible effort to control the shaking in his voice, but suddenly his face crumpled. He rose unsteadily and staggered into the bathroom. When he returned several minutes later, his face was gray and sweat covered his high, bony forehead. Lee-Anna wiped his brow with Kleenex, and she and Theo half led, half carried him to the bedroom.

"Rest, lamb-a-baum," she crooned. "Hush, hush, hush. Forget the dream, poor baby, and rest."

She pulled the sheet to his chin, patted his forehead once again, and together she and Theo tiptoed from the room. Theo bowed slightly toward the closed door and crossed his hands over his chest.

"Surely," he quoted, "I think the wild beasts fear your white bones

Even though you lie there dying, brave Horatio!
Your valor great Pêlion know, and mighty Ossa,
And the wind-swept lonely ways of high Kithairon.

III

"I really feel uncomfortably like Judas Iscariot," Theo confided to Lee-Anna as they slowly descended the rickety steps. "It's awful to betray my luv'," he grimaced and pointed to Roderick who was clinging to his shoulder. As the morning waned, the bantam's condition had deteriorated. His once fierce eyes were glazed, his drooping feathers had become even more bedraggled and were flaked with what appeared to be an incurable case of dandruff.

"Poor Roderick," Lee-Anna said. "Somehow he knows that we have decided to get rid of him. But don't fret, Theo," she added hastily, alarmed at the sudden frown which darkened his face. "You certainly are not solely responsible. This is a group action! Unanimous!"

Beneath her more than usually heavy makeup her heart-shaped face, dramatic beneath an ash-colored shoulder-length wig, was flushed with drink and excitement. She wore her best pale yellow jersey which accentuated her small breasts—you look like a daffodil, Theo had said, a regular Robert Herrick type daffo-downdilly—and walked daintily on dizzily-high spikes, her neat little buttocks beneath the avocado-hued stretch-pants soaring and dipping like a pair of swallows in flight.

"Yes," Theo agreed readily, his face lightening. "It *is* for the best. We will find a home for the foundling, where he will make friends of his own, where he can scream at dusk amidst his fellows, and even, perhaps, eventually find himself a mate."

"Besides," groaned Horatio, somewhat refreshed from his recent nap but shockingly pallid, "this action has been forced upon us."

He paused, breathing heavily, and set down the styrofoam ice chest. Penrod, limping behind him, collapsed awkwardly and rested his shapeless muzzle at Horatio's feet. The poet's long face suddenly wrinkled, grew unbearably tense, and he threw back his balding head and sneezed.

"I have always been allergic to chicken feathers."

"True," Theo acquiesced. He reached towards his shoulder and stroked the bantam's beak. Roderick struggled to rise, and crowed weakly. "In all the excitement last night, we betrayed you, Ray. Forgive our thoughtlessness. As a matter of fact," he added, "it just occurs to me that birds or fowl of any sort are not permitted in faculty housing. So," he concluded, beaming, "none of us is guilty. Come! Come, good friends, it is time for us to depart."

He strode to the car and held the door gallantly for Lee-Anna before assisting Horatio, who had momentarily disappeared behind the car.

"All passion spent," the poet muttered as he sank upon the bumpy rear seat. Theo half-pushed, half-lifted the limp body of Penrod who lay panting on the floor, too exhausted to do more than lick Horatio's sandaled feet. With a wave of his hand, Theo climbed in beside Lee-Anna, who eased the old tired Valiant out of the graveled driveway and onto the chuck-holed road, carefully avoiding the litter of shabby tricycles, dented sand pails, and a sled left over from the late April snow of the preceding month.

"Up, up, and away!" Theo cried as they drove slowly from the compound to the winding blacktop road which led to Highway 63, where rolling bottomlands stretched fat and fallow along the banks of the Missouri River. "And now, dear friends, it will soon be time to wet our jolly whistles."

He fumbled for the styrofoam chest which he had carefully stocked with limes, lemons, cracked ice, dry soda, and light rum.

"Who's for Terrible Theo's special version of fish-house punch?" he chuckled, his spirits rising as the blueish dome of the Administration Building receded in the distance. "Where's the chest, little sweetie?" He patted Lee-Anna's rounded knee fondly.

"It was here a little bit ago," she answered, and

leaned from the window to wave gaily at a small boy on a bicycle. "Children shouldn't ride bikes on the highway," she added absently. "Dangerous."

"Where? What's that?" asked Theo with an edge of irritation in his voice.

"They shouldn't ride bikes on the highway."

"What's that got to do with the chest, honey babe?"

"The chest? What chest?"

"The ice chest with the mixin's. What chest did you think I meant?"

"Oh, the chest. Isn't it in the back with Ray?"

He turned around awkwardly, dislodging Roderick, who tumbled to the seat between them. He glared at Ray, who had fallen asleep, one bony hand resting on Penrod's head.

"Where's the chest, Ray?"

He shook Horatio's shoulder, pushing Penrod aside as the dog swung his shaggy head in his direction. The poet opened his eyes slowly, muttered "The cave with no exit," and again closed his eyes.

"Oh, God in Heaven," Theo cried after carefully scanning the back seat and floor. "The idiot has forgotten the ice chest! Stop the car, Lee-Anna."

As the Valiant lurched to a stop, Horatio again opened his eyes.

"Can't you all be quiet?" His voice was high and querulous. "Can't you see I'm trying to sleep. And keep your hands off Lee-Anna, Theo."

"That's a hell of a way to talk, Ray. Get with it, man, *where* is the chest? In the name of Heaven, what have you done with it?"

"Isn't it up there with you?"

Again Theo searched the front seat.

"No, it isn't here. Good God!"

"Perhaps you put it in the trunk, lamb-a-baum." Lee-Anna's voice was conciliatory.

"Why don't you check it out, Ray?"

"I'm far too weak to check it out, Theo. Far too weak. Why don't you check it out yourself?" Horatio closed his eyes and snuggled close to Penrod, who had struggled from the floor to the seat. "I know," he added in a sepulchral voice; "I expect I left it back at the house."

"That just about tears it," Theo growled. "Let's call the whole thing off. The day's just about ruined, as far as I'm concerned. And stop that damned snuffling, Penrod!"

"You're both impossible!" Lee-Anna folded her arms on the steering wheel, and placed her head in the crook of them, and wept. Penrod raised his head and uttered a low, dismal howl.

"Shut up, Penrod!" Theo leaned over the back of the seat and shook a menacing finger. "Be quiet, sir!"

"Don't tell my dog to shut up, Theo! I suggest you be quiet yourself." Horatio slowly sank back into the inexpensive pillows which Lee-Anna had artfully arranged to cover the worn spots in the upholstery.

Lee-Anna straightened up and frowned at Theo and then at Horatio.

"You're both awful," she said, and fumbled in her straw-and-leather shoulder bag. She withdrew a small linen handerchief, dabbed at the corners of her eyes, and switched on the ignition and slowly eased the car back onto the highway. They drove in silence, the atmosphere heavy with tension and gloom. Penrod lay motionless except for occasional spasmodic twitchings of his bad leg and the flicker of an ear, coffee-dark against the oat-colored curls of his head, and Roderick made no effort to return to his sanctuary on Theo's shoulder but lay grotesquely on the seat beside Lee-Anna.

"Honey babe," Theo said gently after several minutes had passed. "I'm sorry, honey babe."

She did not answer, but stared straight ahead, rigidly confined within an iron maiden of unhappiness. He tentatively patted her thigh, but she made no response but continued to drive slowly along the curving road, oblivious of the clumps of pale green poplars and the gaunt outcroppings of limestone, and the rolling bottomlands which stretched lushly down to the river. He withdrew his hand and grimly lighted a cigarette.

"Oh, Theo," she spoke suddenly, and pulled off the road and stopped the car. Without speaking she turned to him and put her arms around his neck and kissed him on the mouth, deaf to Roderick's protesting squawk. They sat very still for several minutes, her small head on his shoulder.

"I'm sorry, honey babe," Theo said again. "I don't know why we do this."

"I remember!" Horatio struggled to a sitting position on the cluttered back seat. "I *did* put the chest in the trunk! Give me the key, Lee-Anna."

He fumbled with the door, disturbing Penrod, who sighed in his sleep, and staggered from the car. Outside, before going to unlock the trunk, he paused and turned toward Lee-Anna and Theo who, separated, were watching him intently.

"And keep your pickin' hands off Lee-Anna, Theo," he said, and slowly walked to the back of the car and leaned over the trunk with the key in his hand.

IV

In the late afternoon the sky was sherry colored, and spice scented with the breath of hawthorn and apple blossoms. A brown dove perched on the sagging line strung between grayed and weather-aged telephone poles was a talisman of joy, an emblem of hope, a signature for all who had eyes to read—so Theo had exclaimed between long, long draughts from the moisture-beaded Mason jar. Horatio, completely incapacitated by his most recent retching, snored gloomily, his head half buried in Penrod's mane while Roderick, drugged by the warmth and the rhythmic bouncing of the Valiant, dozed uneasily, his toes pressed against Lee-Anna's leg. She had slipped off her shoes; occasionally Theo stroked her crooked little feet, the deformed victims of her penchant for high heels, pausing experimentally to tap the bonelike nail of her third toe.

"A good way to go," he said finally and reached for a cigarette and a kitchen match, and expertly flicked the head with his thumbnail. There was a puff of smoke and a tongue of flame as the head, suddenly snapped from the matchstick, arched through the air to land on the leg of his trousers.

"They don't make kitchen matches the way they used to," he said, and hastily slapped out the widening, fire rimmed circle.

"You kill me," Lee-Anna said, and suddenly they both burst into unrestrained laughter. Quietly he lifted the tail of her jersey from the confining stretch pants and inserted his hands; beneath and above the French bra, her breasts were warm and friendly. They laughed again, like children, and he withdrew his hands and retrieved the Mason jar and held it for her to drink. They continued to drive slowly, and Lee-Anna hummed the lines from Horatio's song, *Yes, you'll bulge at the bel, Nel, bulge at the bel.*

As they rounded a turn, they saw a dingy one-story frame house, a quarter of a mile or so off the road.

"There's a likely-looking home for our princeling." Theo put the Mason jar on the floor. "Surely they must keep chickens."

"If only Andrew Wyeth were here to paint this." Lee-Anna's hand described an arc which included the pale white petals of the stunted hawthorn trees alongside the gravel road, the sparse maples which surrounded the house, and the decrepit, sway-backed outbuildings.

"How about Grandma Moses?" he replied, and took another drink from the jar. "Be of good cheer, Usher, all will be well." He cupped the cock in one hand, its body dry as dust, and trickled a few drops of the spring-well cold liquid into Roderick's half-opened beak. "I shall return," he said to Lee-Anna and stepped from the car. It was farther to the house than he had anticipated, and the stubbled grass was less inviting than it had appeared; he found himself stumbling and once, after recovering his balance, lost sight of the house.

"Turn around," Lee-Anna called from the car; "you're going in the wrong direction."

She started to descend but he waved her away with his free hand.

"No problem," he called hoarsely. "No problem at all, honey babe."

He began the long trek confidently, Roderick clutched firmly in his left hand. The air smelled of scallions; ugh, he thought, and plowed ahead.

At the door, finally, he turned and waved reassuringly in the direction of the car, turned again and knocked, a firm, committed knock. Behind the screen-door, he caught a confused glimpse of an overstuffed sofa and a television set with some kind of brightly painted plaster of paris collie dog. Friendly, good people, he thought; terrible taste, but good solid animal lovers. Then he heard shuffling footsteps, and he was staring through the blurred screen at a woman in a cheap Sears-Roebuck housedress, hair like iron filings, and a squint.

She stared at him, neither hostile nor friendly, the blank stare of a heifer.

"Yes?" she said, finally.

"Good evening, ma'am." Theo's voice was rich, rum-illuminated, reassuring. "Excuse my intruding like this, but I have a favor to ask of you." He exhaled ingratiatingly, and the woman took a hasty backward step. "Or, rather, ma'am, I have a gift for you."

"Uh?"

"Yes, dear friend, a gift." He pointed to Roderick, motionless in the crook of his left arm, and tried to ignore the look of confusion and hostility which was slowly spreading over the pasty countenance behind the screen.

"Do you, ma'am, keep chickens?" With a slight bow he pointed to the drooping figure of the cock.

Without speaking the woman turned and disappeared into the shadows of the house. Theo waited patiently, and hummed the stirring rhythms of the "Ode to Joy." How fortunate, he thought, leaning against the door jamb, that woman is. Here she is, buried in the country—he peered mistily at the scrubby grass, the still leafless pin oaks, and browned-out cedars—and suddenly out of the blue, as it were, a talented stranger—he straightened his slumping shoulders and threw back his head—knocks at the door and offers a bounty. A prize cock who may bring them a little extra money—he flicked Roderick's limp comb with his forefinger—and, indeed, a companionship she has never before experienced.

He heard heavy footsteps: a man stood before him, a pale, lean man dressed in overalls, with pale, lean eyes and a slight tic at the corner of his mouth.

Obviously spastic, Theo thought. With an effort he pushed himself free of the wall of the house and bowed in the direction of the lean man.

"Good day, sir!" How rich and warm my voice sounds, he thought. "Here is the cock, sir, about which I recently spoke to your wife. Yours for the taking, sir. Give him a good home; he richly deserves it, and will amply repay your kindness."

He inclined his head toward Roderick, consciously straining until the two blurred bantam heads merged into one.

"The hour of parting has come, old friend." He tightened his hand around the thin chest and extended his arm in the direction of the thin man.

"Here, sir," he began, slowly trying to focus his eyes.

The sagging porch was vacant. Theo stood uncertainly, Roderick's limp and lusterless tail feathers drooping and spilling between the fingers of his outstretched hand. Theo found himself counting the paint-flecked, uneven floorboards when again he was aware of the sound of heavy footsteps. Painfully he raised his head: he was looking up at the barrrel of a shotgun. Slowly, inexorably, the steel cylinder descended until Theo found himself staring into the empty blue eye of the muzzle.

"No!" he cried. He turned quickly, Roderick tumbling from his hand. With ineffable dignity he stooped to retrieve the limp body. Only then, slowly and majestically, did he retreat from the porch to stumble across the field towards the car. Lee-Anna, breathless and barefooted, her shoulders shaking with unrelieved laughter, gingerly picked her way across the stubble to meet him.

V

"I am a-weary of all this good Samaritan jazz, darling," Theo sighed. "The days of gracious gift-giving and gift-receiving are past." He lay resignedly on the coarse oat-colored Mexican blanket which Lee-Anna had spread out on a slightly rising grass-covered bank a few feet from the Valiant; he traced with a drooping forefinger the pyramid-shaped designs of gray, green, and black, before reaching out for Lee-Anna's hand. In the west, great scarlet fingers of cloud probed the lemon-colored sky; somewhere behind a clump of cottonwoods a cow lowed mournfully, and the scent of new green growth from the fields hovered in the still air like the recollection of a child's hasty kiss. In the cramped back seat of the car Horatio turned uneasily in his sleep, half-raised his head from Penrod's curly shoulder. "The cave with no exit, the cave with no exit," he muttered, and slumped back into disturbed dreams.

Lee-Anna withdrew a cigarette from her jeweled case and leaned over Theo.

"We have done the best we can," she said, glancing at the limp body of Roderick beside Theo, motionless except for an occasional shudder.

Theo nodded, and extended a lighted match. She cupped his hand in both of hers and raised the flame toward her mouth like a bishop bearing a chalice to some high altar. She drew deeply, and exhaled gratefully.

"You are a darling," she said, and sank down beside him. They lay very quietly for several minutes while the firm outline of the scarlet fingers blurred and dissolved into a pink and lavendar haze above the dark fringe of earth; a chill crept into the air and a slight mist rose from the hollows.

Theo ran his fingers lightly around Lee-Anna's throat.

"Let's have one more drink, and then go home."

He returned to the car and slopped the remains of the rum and soda over the diminished ice in the Mason jar. Swirling the mixture gently, listening to the lap-lap-lap of the fragrant drink against the sides of the jar, he suddenly felt at peace with the world; without thinking, he leaned over the seat and placed his hand on Horatio's knee. The poet stirred uneasily before resuming the heavy, labored breathing of the asthmatic. Theo was raising the Mason jar to his lips when he heard the cry from Lee-Anna.

"Theo," she called. "Theo, hurry, something terrible is happening."

The Mason jar slipped from between his hands, the punch drenching the crotch of his rumpled trousers, and trickling coldly down his leg. He ran from the car and knelt beside Lee-Anna. Roderick lay on his back, his egg-yolk toes slowly contracting and expanding; in the thinning light they looked like the plastic feet of the artificial Easter chickens in the dime stores. His pale dented beak was agape, his eyes coated with a scummy film. As Theo reached over to touch the scrawny body, Roderick shuddered and uttered a hoarse, feeble cry; he made one convulsive effort to regain his feet, and fluttered his wings and fell back. Theo touched his hand to Lee-Anna's head and walked back to the car and sat down in the front seat where Penrod had crawled to the floorboards and was thirstily lapping the muddied remains of the fishhouse punch.

"Roderick's dead," Theo said to Horatio, who did not hear him. He withdrew the plastic half-pint flask of whiskey he always kept in the glove compartment of the Valiant, and took a short swallow. Then he returned to Lee-Anna, who was sitting on the blanket, and sat down beside her without speaking. She had placed Roderick's body in her lap and was looking at the last faint gray smudges of the sunset. He removed one of her hands from her lap and placed it in his own. She made no effort to remove it, and he stroked her palm gently with his fingertips, and clumsily put his arm around her shoulder; her flesh was cold beneath his touch. He took off his rumpled jacket and draped it around her shoulders, and kissed her lightly on the cheek. They sat quietly for a few minutes, the coolness rising in the dusk like water. Finally, he touched her elbow, and she half rose and lifted Roderick's body from her lap and placed it on the ground beside the coarse fringes of the Mexican blanket. He squatted alongside the blanket and with his heel and some sticks and a sharp pointed stone dug a shallow grave and placed the body in it. When he had covered it with dirt and pebbles, he rose and stretched. His knees were stiff and the calves of his legs ached. He folded the blanket carefully and returned to the car and opened the trunk and put the blanket away. He returned to Lee-Anna, and put his arm around her waist and together they walked back to the car and sat down on the uncomfortable front seat. He offered her the whiskey flask, but she shook her head.

Horatio slowly opened his eyes and patted Penrod's head; the dog lay on the seat beside him, his beard damp from the remains of the fishhouse punch.

"It's time to go back," Theo said, and turned the ignition key.

"Okay," Horatio said, and closed his eyes.

"Roderick's dead," Lee-Anna said.

"Dead?"

"He died, and Theo buried him."

"Poor little chap." Horatio closed his eyes and lay back.

They drove home slowly. The car was again quiet except for Horatio's breathing and an occasional hiccup from Penrod. When, finally, they turned onto Ashland Gravel Road and could see the glowing banks of light from the Medical Center and the pale luminescent spires of the Union Building, Lee-Anna placed her hand in Theo's lap. He drove with extreme caution as they approached the faculty compound where children were still playing on the two-by-four lawns of the crackerbox houses. Three little girls were singing "London Bridge Is Falling Down," their untrained voices clear and fra-

gile and pure in the darkness. Theo turned the Valiant
into Horatio and Lee-Anna's driveway, and stopped the
car; she withdrew her hand, and placed it gently on his
knee. Then, together, they helped Horatio and Penrod
from the car and up the rickety steps and through the
living room where on the sides and rims of the Bloody
Mary glasses the flecks of tomato juice had hardened
into cement-like flecks and blotches, and the smell of
stale cigarette smoke still lingered in the air. They de-
posited Horatio on the bed, and Theo gently removed
his shoes and loosened his tie while Lee-Anna washed
his hands and face with a dampened washrag. They
pulled the light blanket up to his chin and lowered the
shade and switched on the nightlight on the wall beside
the bed. Then they tiptoed out of the room, gingerly
stepping over the snoring mass of Penrod's limp body,
and closed the flimsy door behind them. Theo mixed a
pair of whiskeys and water while Lee-Anna brewed a
pot of coffee. They sat down together on the sofa-bed,
and sipped their coffee and drank their whiskeys, and
smoked.

"It's been a long day," Lee-Anna said, and turned
her face to him and kissed him. Very gently he removed
her earrings before he slipped off her jersey. His fingers
were clumsy, and he had difficulty trying to unhook the
lacy French bra, and she put her left hand to her back
in a skilled and accustomed manner and deftly un-
hooked it and slipped it from her and dropped it to the
floor. He unzipped her avocado stretchpants, now a
blurred gray in the unlighted room, and leaned over
her; she arched her body slightly, raising her little buttocks from the rumpled sheets, and he withdrew the
stretchpants, but made no effort to touch the wispy bi-

kini beneath them. He took off his shoes and lay down beside her.

"It's been a good day," he said. He put his arm around her, seeking one warm round little breast. She put her mouth against his and they sat quietly together, without speaking or moving, while outside the sounds of the children diminished and then faded away completely, and the sky blackened over the blurred mass of the university buildings.